Frederick William Robinson

Wrayford's Ward, and Other Tales

Frederick William Robinson

Wrayford's Ward, and Other Tales

ISBN/EAN: 9783337137076

Printed in Europe, USA, Canada, Australia, Japan

Cover: Foto ©Andreas Hilbeck / pixelio.de

More available books at **www.hansebooks.com**

WRAYFORD'S WARD,

AND OTHER TALES.

BY

F. W. ROBINSON,

AUTHOR OF

"GRANDMOTHER'S MONEY,"

&c. &c.

IN THREE VOLUMES.

VOL. I.

LONDON:

HURST AND BLACKETT, PUBLISHERS,

13, GREAT MARLBOROUGH STREET.

1872.

LONDON:
PRINTED BY MACDONALD AND TUGWELL, BLENHEIM HOUSE,
BLENHEIM STREET, OXFORD STREET.

WRAYFORD'S WARD.

NOTICE.

It having been found, after these volumes were printed, that a work called " A Girl's Romance" was published a few years since, it has been thought desirable to alter the title of the first story from " A Girl's Romance" to " Wrayford's Ward."

WRAYFORD'S WARD:

A GIRL'S ROMANCE.

CHAPTER I.

"OLD WRAYFORD."

HE was called Old Wrayford before he was seven-and-thirty years of age. His habits were old-fashioned; he was an old-fashioned, studious-looking man, and what else could be expected? The people of Greymoor had no fine feelings of their own, and did not profess to understand fine feelings in other folk; they were not great judges of age, perhaps, and Abel Wrayford was older than his looks, hence it was always "Old Wrayford" in common conversation. He did not like the title—he had been heard to express himself a little

querulously at it, by one who brightened
his home, and him ; but the name had
been bestowed as if by general agreement,
and there was no changing it in Greymoor.
Greymoor was a place where nicknames
clung to one.

Well, he looked " Old Wrayford," especially from a few yards distant, when he
was proceeding along thoughtfully, with his
head very much craned forwards, as if
the weight of his new ideas were a trifle
too much for it. He did not resemble
a man of seven-and-thirty then—his steps
were slow and measured, and he had a habit
of walking, pantaloon fashion, with one arm
crossed behind him, as if to prop his back
up during his progress ; he was high-
shouldered with hard study of chemicals
and books, and with much " writing-work "
for scientific periodicals in London, where
he was better known than in this wild
Cornish village that he loved ; he was grey-
haired even. He was tall and thin, and his

face was lined beyond his years; only his eyes betokened light and life, for they were clear, bright, grey eyes, full of fire and power still. He had studied all his youth away; he had stepped aside from youth's frivolities, and given himself up to a science which ages its true votaries early, as a rule, and to this rule Abel Wrayford was no exception. He was very young at heart; an earnest, simple-minded, clever, blundering creature, knowing nothing of the world itself, and but little of his fellow-beings; a man who thought the best of everybody, and gave everybody credit for the best intentions.

He had lived at Greymoor almost all his life. Friends had told him long ago that in London he would find prosperity and fame; but he had a horror of cities, and his was a mind which was contented with a little. He had been to London fifteen years ago, and the place had unsettled him, and made him ill—he had suffered from fever there, and when his strength returned he had been glad to get back to his Cornish home. It had been his father's home before him, and here he could study in peace, with nothing more to disturb him than the wash of the sea against the rocks in the Cove, a hundred feet below him, and not a hundred yards away. His father had died poor, and there did not seem any probability of Abel Wrayford becoming a rich man. He was fond of experiments, and the money which he earned in writing a treatise, or expounding a theory for the *Scientific Register*, was sure to be spent in new apparatus, or in following out a new idea—very often a fallacious one, despite his cleverness. Had it not been for his ward, he would have even drifted into debt, after the fashion of such thoughtless, dreamy beings as he all the world over; but she ruled his house and home, and was a practical young woman in her way.

Of this ward it is necessary to speak ere

we commence our story proper. Grace
Edmonds became his ward, housekeeper,
and general manager at the early age of
nine. Her father had been the senior of
Abel Wrayford by three or four years, and
Abel Wrayford, who had left his father's
home early, went into partnership with his
friend Edmonds, and lived with him at
Launceston, until Edmonds, who had married early in life, found children increasing rapidly about him. Wrayford went
once more to Launceston to help his friend,
and be of comfort to him, when a terrible
epidemic, which had raged through England, swept away Edmond's wife, and three
children out of four that had blessed a
happy but brief marriage. Here Wrayford
remained with his old friend for two more
years, and then Edmonds, who had been
long ailing, broke up suddenly, enjoining
his friend with his last breath to see to
Grace, and be to her all that he would have
been himself, had it been God's will to

spare him. He died possessed of five-and-twenty pounds, which he left in trust to Abel Wrayford until his little girl came of age; and he adjoined to that trust a sentimental, even a foolish request that Grace was never to marry without the consent of her guardian, on whose judgment, good feeling, and generosity he knew that he could rely. It was a mere wish, involving no pains and penalty, no forfeiture of the little legacy—merely a simple expression of his confidence in the guardian whom he had appointed, and a hint to Grace, as she grew older, where he thought she would find her best friend and truest adviser. Perhaps he was the only one in the world who thoroughly understood Abel Wrayford, but he had been like Abel's big brother at school, and they had been staunch friends through life together.

Abel was a young guardian, but his father and mother were living when he took Edmond's child back to his Cornish home, and bade them help him with his trust, which they did cheerfully and willingly, as though Grace had been a child of their own. They both died before Grace was a woman, and Grace had been Wrayford's fairy house-keeper some years when our story opens on them. She was close on eighteen years of age, and he had passed his seven-and-thirtieth Summer, and was "old Wray-ford" to the world of Greymoor—old Wrayford to his ward also, for she called him father, and saw in him almost the father whom she had lost. He was proud of the title which her love had given him, and often called her his child, and there was no one in the world so near to his heart as she was. The people in the village below them—for Wrayford's house was perched high up amongst the rocks—called her Miss Wrayford more often than Miss Edmonds, and thought her life must be a very dull and lonely one with that grey-haired, grave man whose soul was in

his studies, and whose lamp, like a danger-
signal in the topmost room, burned always
far into the night.

CHAPTER II.

THE NEW CRAZE AND THE NEW-COMER.

WHEN an idea entered Abel Wrayford's head—and he was always beset by ideas which interfered with his legitimate work—it was Grace's laughing fashion to call it his new craze; and late in the keen November month when our story opens on this chemist's life, a new craze had suddenly seized on him. It came to him in the evening, when the sea was rough, and broke in thunderous masses upon the shingle below, when the wind rioted without and shook the house, and the rain was hurled in sheets upon the old-fashioned lattice windows. A bitter night for a bright warm fancy, which danced before the eyes of the student like a truth within a hand's grasp. He had been writing an article on colour for the *Register* in his little wainscoted sitting-room, the result of an analysis which he had prosecuted in his laboratory upstairs that very afternoon; and Grace was humming blithely to herself by the fireside, happy in his silent company, and not disturbing him in his essay—for Abel was used to her musical variations, and even affirmed he liked them, and worked at his best if she were not studying his peace—when the thought came to him. The pen ceased to travel over the paper, the eyes took a steady survey of the opposite wall, the thin white hand took a firm clutch of the chin, and he began to mutter to himself in an insane manner, not particularly exhilarating to an observer, even to one like Grace, who knew his idiosyncrasies pretty well.

" What is the matter, Gardy ?"

"Hush, my dear—don't disturb me," he said, in a low voice.

"Is it a new idea?" she asked, in a low tone, to match his own, taking up the key-note which he had struck.

"Yes, I think so. An idea, Grace, which might lead to fortune, if it were grasped at once, and there were no flaws to mar its successful issue."

"Oh! but you have had so many ideas of that kind," Grace gently hinted; "and there have been many flaws in them, which have led us a long way out of the right road."

"Yes, as you say," he answered, absently; "but don't talk to me just now."

Grace was silent after this entreaty. She bent her head over her work, and feigned to be industrious, glancing now and then at her grey-haired, pale-faced guardian, and wishing, in her heart, that he would turn to the pages of his manuscript. Quarter-day was close upon them, and she knew that there had not been much cash set

aside for it, much money saved for it, Abel
having been more theoretical and less practical than usual during the last two months.
The house had recently changed hands,
also, and Grace would have liked to look
well with the new landlord as a start off,
especially as that landlord was Robert
Trustworth, a master-fisherman in the village, who had saved much money of late
years, and bought much property in the
neighbourhood, and of whom Grace would
not have liked to ask a favour, as she had
often done of her former landlord. But
Abel Wrayford was not thinking of land-
lords, the Christmas quarter's rent, or the
article for next month's *Scientific Register*,
and he continued to stare before him until
even his fair ward grew a little anxious.

" How the wind blows to-night!" she said
at last ; and he answered, still absently,

" Yes; don't touch it, Grace," and frightened her a little more. She was thinking of
calling his attention to the pages crumpled

beneath his elbow as a last resource, when he suddenly jumped to his feet, and clutched the table-lamp before him.

"I shall not be long," he said. "A minute or two—not more." He went rapidly to his top-room, wherein he locked himself, away from her, and, in his absence of mind, left her in the darkness downstairs, until she lighted a fresh lamp for herself, and sat patiently awaiting his return, scarcely hoping to see him again that evening, and knowing too well where his new craze was likely to lead him.

He came down, however, in an hour's time, looking rather wild, with his grey-shot locks rubbed all manner of ways, and laughing heartily as at a pleasant joke with which some familiar upstairs had favoured him. He took a place in front of the fire, spread his hands before the blaze, and gave vent to one incomprehensible word—

"Mud!"

Grace repeated the word, and looked at

him wonderingly.   He met her glance, and laughed again.

"Yes, it was really a craze, Grace," he said.   "I thought that I had discovered a new colour, a bran-span bright and daz‑zling tint, and the result was mud, my dear. That is all."

"You will not work any more to-night?" she asked.

"No," he replied, after a glance at his papers.   "Lock up my desk, child, and put my papers away, like a careful amanuen‑sis as you are.   That was a strange fancy to get into my head about a colour.   I never had such an idea before, and it was very ridiculous of me, just as I was in full swing at my article, too.   But one is led astray now and then from the right track, and the hours waste themselves sadly.   Did you say that the wind was howling very much to-night?"

"I said so before you went upstairs to your study," was the quiet answer.

"Ah! I know you mentioned it. Yes, it comes full swoop at us from the sea, and moans, like some one wounded and sore, outside the house. An uncomfortable night."

"Gardy," said Grace suddenly, turning very white, "there is something moaning outside the house beside the wind to-night."

"The deuce there is!" replied Abel Wrayford, rising with his ward. "I hope you may be wrong."

Grace had already risen, drawn aside the heavy window-curtains, and looked out at the night's darkness, and Abel took his place beside her in the same watchful attitude. On the alert for something strange and eventful, they did not appear greatly surprised when a cry of help, as from the beach below the cliff on which Wrayford's house was built, welled faintly to their ears. Grace turned a shade paler, perhaps, and laid her hand upon her guardian's shoulder.

"Did I not say so?" she asked.

"Certainly you did. My hat and stick, my dear—the lantern from the downstairs room—I'll go and see if I can be of help. I hope it's not another wreck."

Grace brought him his hat and stick, and the lighted lantern which he had asked for. He did not observe that she was dressed for walking too until he was at the door.

"Why, Grace!"

"I would rather go with you," she said; "I may be of use to some poor sufferer cast upon the beach."

"But——"

She would not listen to his reasoning. She shut herself outside with him in the wind and rain, which came at them tempestuously, and extinguished the light in the lantern to begin with.

"My dear, you must go back," said Abel, solicitously. "I had no conception that it was such an awful night, and you are young, and delicate, and unfit for storms."

"Some one is abroad and in danger," she

said, " and I will go along with you. You
are too near-sighted to venture near the cliff
without me."

"Oh! that's nonsense," he answered;
" my sight improves, and—— Why, Grace,
look there! Something is moving at the
edge of the cliff, crawling towards us, or the
night deceives me. We shall not have far
to go."

Guardian and ward hurried towards the
figure moving on the brink, as it were, of
the precipice, and a man's voice called to
them as they approached. An instant afterwards, and Abel Wrayford's grasp had
saved the man from falling backwards to
the beach again.

" How came you here?—what is it?—
are there any more below?"

The man replied in French, " No one
else," and fainted away. Abel Wrayford
and his ward bore him with difficulty to
their house, seated him before the fire in
their warm parlour, and used every effort

to restore him to consciousness. Presently his hand wandered to his forehead, as though he were trying to remember something in his sleep, and those who were bending over him knew that he was coming to himself.

He was a young man of three or four-and-twenty years, dark and handsome, his white hands and his short, silky, black moustache a great deal at variance with the sailor's dress he wore. He opened his eyes, looked round him wildly for an instant, and then glanced from Abel Wrayford to his ward.

"Friends?" he asked, in English this time.

"Yes, friends, of course," replied Wrayford.

"English people?" he said slowly.

Abel again replied in the affirmative.

"You are always hospitable—I thank you for your solicitude," he said, with a strong foreign accent. "I shall be better in a few minutes, and will not trouble you longer than I can help. You will allow me to rest for half an hour, I am sure."

"Half an hour!" said Wrayford—"you must stay here all night, man, unless you want to risk your life again. You must go to bed at once, and we will dry your clothes by the morning."

"You are very kind," he murmured; "but——"

"But you must let us have our way," said Wrayford, cheerily; "you are not the first sailor who has been dried by Abel Wrayford's fire. We are used to wrecks on this part of the coast."

"I thank you very much," he answered, gratefully; "but if you will allow me, I would rather proceed upon my journey—I am anxious to reach London. I am a very —poor—man."

He made the confession reluctantly, addressing Grace rather than her guardian, as though from a woman he anticipated more of sympathy for his forlorn condition.

She looked towards Abel Wrayford quickly, as he concluded, and Abel understood her glance.

"You do us an injustice in your thoughts, young man," he said, gravely; "poverty or riches will make no difference in our treatment of the stranger cast upon our shores."

"You will allow me first to explain how it is that I am in this condition, and then——"

"I will see you into bed, and hear all explanations afterwards," said Wrayford, sturdily; "man, do not you know that you are wet through—and spoiling my carpet with salt water," he added, drily.

Wrayford was a charitable and deep-feeling man, it was evident—close study of his profession, and little communion with his race, had not narrowed his heart nor rendered him ascetic. Human suffering always touched him; and the troubles of his fellow-men were certain to arouse his sympathy. The Frenchman was impressed by this geni-

ality, and would have overwhelmed him
with thanks, had the chemist allowed it; but
Abel was determined on getting the damp
stranger to his room, in which an active
maid-servant had already lighted a fire.
The stranger went up a few stairs with some
confidence, then paused, and motioned Abel
Wrayford to his side.

"I am weaker than I thought," he said,
faintly—"I am in great pain."

"Where?"

"Here in my left side—I am afraid, good
friend, that I must trouble you for a doctor."

Wrayford got him to his room, and into
his bed, and then went in search of the
doctor, as the stranger had desired.

"This is rather an awkward lodger who
has dropped upon us, Grace," he said, before
he started on his errand—"one who will be
an expense, and who has told us frankly
that he has nothing wherewith to reimburse
us for our outlay; but we will make the
best of him."

" Poor fellow !—he seems very ill."

"I am afraid he is," replied Wrayford.
"I wonder if he has any friends in France
or England to whom we can write. I will
ask him when I come back."

The French stranger was not able to
give him an answer upon his return with
the doctor—he was tossing in his bed, and
singing the " Marseillaise " so very much out
of tune that every drop of blood in Grace and
the servant's body had become curdled by
the discord. He had passed away from the
consciousness of present surroundings, and
was fighting with fever, and with a madness
born of fever. He raved in French a great
deal of his country, a little of his mother,
whom he spoke as of one away from him in
Paris ; he anathematised tyrants, and he
called down vengeance on a government
which had cast him down; and then he
dashed into his " Marseillaise " again, and
sang it worse than ever.

" This is a bad case," said the doctor.

"How did he get here, Mr. Wrayford?"

"Well, he came like Jonah—from the sea," said Wrayford, drily; "and that is all I know about him."

"Well off, I should say?" was the next remark.

"Poor as Job," answered Wrayford, who was great in Scriptural parallels that evening.

"You do not mean that?" affirmed the doctor. "Why, the man will not recover, and who is to settle my account?"

"I will settle that," replied Wrayford; adding to himself, "but who is to settle with the undertaker, the Lord knows!"

"I believe that he will soon be better," said Grace, a short time afterwards; and she was a truer prophet than the doctor. A woman very often is.

CHAPTER III.

THE CONVALESCENT.

VICTOR DUFOY—for such was the name of the young gentleman who had introduced himself, damp and dripping, into the chemist's quiet home—recovered in due course, though he took his time about it, and kept his new friends in suspense concerning his movements—towards life or the grave—for several weeks.

He had broken a rib, he had taken to himself an unpleasant fever, and there were bad symptoms setting in; but in the face of these difficulties, and thanks to the care of Abel Wrayford and his ward, he fought his way back to the world. It was close on

Christmas Day, when he was enabled to come downstairs, sit by the fireside, and be pronounced out of danger. He received the congratulations of Abel and Grace as he sat before the fire in Mr. Wrayford's dressing-gown, wherein he had made himself at home, after a few protestations against the confiscation, all of which had been over-ruled—and he hastened to reply.

"I do not know how I shall be able to re-pay you for your kindness," he said, warmly. "Scarcely am I able to thank you enough for past and present care of me. Without you both I must have died."

"And now that you are living and rational —for you have been talking the most absurd nonsense for weeks—perhaps you will tell us who you are, and how you came here?" said Wrayford.

"Cheerfully," he answered. "It is a long story, and will try your patience a little."

"Keep to the facts, and we shall soon get through them," said Wrayford, encourag-

ingly. " And remember that divergence is
an infliction."

Wrayford was in high spirits at Victor's
recovery, and probably at the prospect of
getting him out of the house safe and sound.
His last article in the *Scientific Register* had
been a success also, and the papers had
been talking of it, praising and attacking
it, after their several fashions ; and a reply
had been called for from Abel Wrayford's
pen, which was at work at the present
moment, in his defence of that particular
theory as regarded colour which had nearly
set him off after another *ignis fatuus.* He
had earned more money than usual that
month, for he had been more than usually
industrious, and the quarter's rent would
have been put by for Mr. Trustworth, the
new landlord, had it not been for the sick
man and his wants. Abel wrote his article, and
professed to be listening to the young man's
account of himself at the same time ; he
only caught the salient points of the story,

but as the narrator diverged horribly—Abel
was sure that he would do it, despite his
warning—there was not a great deal lost.
Grace Edmonds would hear every word,
and would be able to throw a clearer light
on matters of detail, if required. She did
not tire of Victor Dufoy's animated description of the sufferings of his beloved France,
of his fierce struggle with a maniacal few
to redress her wrongs, of his misfortunes
and failures, and his hurried escape from
his country, leaving his mother in Paris.
It was the old story of the patriot in difficulties, ending in much the same way as
the red shirt and blue blouse generally end,
only Victor had undergone a few perils
at sea, by way of a wind up. He had left
France, where it had grown too hot to
hold him, in a fishing-smack, that had trans-
ferred him to another fishing-smack, English
bound, which had been caught in a strong
gale, and thrown out of its course, and
which, in making for a Cornish harbour,

that November night, whereon he was found
first, had contrived to pitch him—owing to his
indifferent sea-legs—overboard when sight-
ing shore. Victor had managed to swim in
the darkness to land, and battle his way
through the surf to Greymoor Cove, and rest
on the beach panting for awhile, and wondering where he was. There he became
convinced that the tide was advancing fast
upon him, and that he was hemmed in by
a semicircle of rugged cliffs; and taking Abel
Wrayford's light in the top-room window for
a beacon, he climbed his way towards it,
praying for his life, and reaching the summit
at last, minus one rib, which had been since
patched up by a Cornish doctor very suc-
cessfully.

" May I inquire what was your profession
before you took to politics?" said Wrayford.

"Certainly," was the answer; " I was a
student of chemistry."

" How strange !" said Grace.

"Ah! it would have been better to stick to the profession," said the chemist, "there are less dangerous explosions to be feared from our gases than from the meeting of opposing political atoms. Where did you study—what did you learn—under whom did you practice—what do you know?"

Abel was more interested in his friend's scientific acquirements than in his red-republican tenets, and he set aside his work to cross-examine the convalescent. He found that Victor knew more of chemistry than he had given him credit for knowing, that the Frenchman was wrong in many things which he had learned, but that it would not take a great deal of trouble to set him right; for he was shrewd and clever, and somewhat of a thinker for himself.

Abel Wrayford took a greater interest in Victor Dufoy from this day; he discovered in him a companion who was of service, and as Victor grew stronger, the chemist even began

to think that he should be sorry to lose him
presently. Thus Christmas faded into the
new year, and still found Victor a guest at
Abel Wrayford's table.

It was time for Dufoy to take his departure at last. He had been six weeks at
Greymoor, and the place had grown more
like home to him than he cared to reflect
upon—it pained him deeply to think of
leaving it. Abel Wrayford and Grace had
both been very kind, more than kind, and
his was a heart that had been touched by
their generosity. Abel had been as an
elder brother to him, and Grace more like
his sister than a stranger, and in all England
besides he had not one friend. He did not
see his way clearly to a means of living in
England; he had come over very poor; he
and his mother had been poor for years,
owing to the sequestration of an estate
which had belonged to their family; and in
England he was friendless as well as penniless. He was a proud man too, and it

wounded him deeply to know that he must leave Wrayford in debt—in debt as to money that was due, and which he was unable to pay. All this on his mind, and a something more perhaps which he did not care to give voice to, or bestow more thought than he could help upon, and he going away from Greymoor! Well, the sooner the better, though his heart sank very much when he fixed the day, and told Wrayford that he should leave on the Friday.

"And if I can repay back to you all the past kindness, dear friend," he cried, "if my family step into its rights, and I am less the slave of circumstances, yours shall be the first house to which I will come, asking you and your ward to rejoice with me over my good fortune. I think—that is, I hope, that I shall be able to repay your kindness some day."

Later that day—it was the day before Victor's departure—when Wrayford and his ward were alone, the former said suddenly,

"I shall be sorry to lose Victor; he is a
modest young fellow, and he has been of
service to me.   It will take time to get over
his absence."

Grace knew that Abel Wrayford was
watching her very intently as he spoke—
looking at her from his desk in the corner,
as though he were anxious to learn if she
was sorry too that Victor was going away.
She was more sorry than she was aware
of herself at that time; but she did not
care to show any regret for the departure of the young Frenchman, even to so
old a friend as Abel was.   She had not ana-
lyzed her feelings respecting Victor Dufoy;
and as Victor had simply seemed to regret
the home he was quitting, and the kindness
he was leaving behind him—not the people
so much—it was not her place to affect any
particular regret.   Besides, she was a woman, and her womanly instinct was to hide
her real sentiments for the present; and if
Victor did not care about his going away—

that is, for losing sight of her—for ever, too !
—why, it was not very likely that she was
going to cry her eyes out for him, or at
least let anybody think—not even her dear,
old-fashioned, faithful guardian—that she
was indulging in that process surreptitiously.

"I suppose we shall miss him," she said
carelessly.

"Perhaps he will go back to France,
and marry the young lady whom his mother has in store for him," said Abel Wrayford.

"Oh ! is there a young lady in store for
him over there ?" asked Grace, more carelessly, although she worked a little more
energetically as she made the inquiry.

Wrayford was near-sighted, and did not
notice this.

"So he tells me—a cousin of his, with
the same blood in her veins, and who has
been marked out for him from the time that
he was ten years old."

"And he likes her, of course ?"

"He thinks that he shall like her in time; his mother is sure that he will," said Wrayford.

"I don't admire such a match as that!" said Grace.

"Why not? It is the best of matches in its way. The young folk have time to understand each other—to grow up together, believing and trusting in each other. There is nothing hasty or foolish about it, Grace."

"No; but it is very unromantic," replied Grace.

"Are you romantic?" he asked, very anxiously. But Grace's merry laugh at his suspicions re-assured him, and he bent down with a smile over his manuscript again. He was glad that Grace was not romantic, but looked at life seriously and methodically; and he was more than glad that she was not as sorry to part with Victor Dufoy as . he was. Convinced of this, reading his ward's heart like an open book—it had always been easy to read, for she was free from guile, and had not a secret from him, and she never would have, he was assured —he mooted another idea which had been troubling him that morning.

" I have been thinking, Grace, whether it is not possible to render Victor's stay in Greymoor profitable to him and me."

" Is that another craze, Gardy ?" asked Grace, very demurely.

" No, I don't think it is," he replied ; " for Victor is useful, and the only question is, whether there is work enough for the two of us. There is a great deal of my work that he can take off my hands, leaving me free to write more often, or to go off more frequently on those wild-goose chimeras at which you jest so pleasantly."

" We will say to write more frequently ; for write you must, Abel," said Grace, gravely. "I have been going to tell you that the rent——"

" Yes, yes—I know all about that," said Abel, interrupting her ; " it is just due, and

I am not so well prepared for it as I should be. But Robert Trustworth is a rich man, and will not come running after his money at twelve o'clock on quarter-day."

"And if he should, there is twenty-five po——"

"No, there is not," said Abel, sharply, and looking so firm and hard at the suggestion that Grace did not allude further to that expedient. She returned to the old question, and was grave and demure enough to have deceived Argus himself.

"And is it wise, with fresh difficulties ahead of us, to talk of an assistant, Gardy?" she asked. "Had not the young man better go his way?"

"No, I think not," he replied; "for he will give me time to myself; and I want time immensely. And as for difficulties, I will smite them down, expunge them from the face of our daily life in less than a week, my dear."

"Very well, guardian—you know best."

Grace said no more, but went about her work cheerfully—went down into the village of Greymoor, after seeing Victor and her guardian in conference together in the parlour, and gave her orders for the next week's housekeeping, and that day's dinner, with her usual alacrity. She was in high, bright spirits it was observed by the shopkeepers, and full of cheery gossip with the villagers; and as she was generally light and bright,—the sunshine of the place, as of Abel Wrayford's home,—it was strange that her manner should have been especially remarked that morning. Stranger still that she was not aware that her spirits were brighter and lighter, and that she would not have acknowledged the fact had she been questioned concerning it. Indeed, she had risen with a dull heart and a headache, she was sure, that very day; and only her high spirit had thrown off the depression. She went up the ascent to Abel Wrayford's home, and found Victor Dufoy standing on the edge of the cliff, looking out to sea, with his arms folded, very much like a certain illustrious exile and Frenchman whose portrait we have seen very often. He was so absorbed in thought, that he was not aware of Grace's presence until she touched him lightly on the arm.

"Oh! I beg pardon," he said; "I did not know that you were here."

"You are looking very cross, Mr. Dufoy," she said; "I do not think that I have intruded on pleasant thoughts, and so I hope that I am sure of your forgiveness."

"No, they were not pleasant thoughts," he answered, almost without looking at her.

"Nothing has happened to disturb you, I hope?"

"N—no—nothing particular," he said. "I am going away from my new friends— the only friends whom I possess in England —and am not in good spirits. There, I confess it."

" But——"

And Grace paused, and looked at him steadily, and with the faintest increase of colour on her pretty face. He waited patiently for her to continue, and she said,

" But have you not seen my guardian?— has he not asked you to stay and assist him for awhile?"

"He has asked me, Miss Grace, and I have refused."

" Refused!" she repeated, in amazement. "For what reason?"

" I would prefer your not asking me my reasons," he said, folding his arms, and looking out to sea again *à la* Bonaparte.

" Very well, Mr. Dufoy," she said; " it is no business of mine, of course. If you are tired of us, it is natural to go away."

She wished that she had not uttered those words the instant after they had escaped her; but it was too late. He looked quickly from the sweep of ocean, flecked by a myriad of golden ripples that bright Winter's morning, and turned with eagerness towards her. She began to quicken her pace in the direction of the house, but his rapid strides soon brought him up with her.

"For what reason, you asked me a moment since, Miss Edmonds," he said, in a hoarse, agitated voice—"perhaps it is fairer to tell you. Because you have all been too kind and generous towards a poor refugee— because I am too happy."

"I—I do not understand you."

"It is better for me that I go—it is my duty to yourself and Mr. Wrayford. I should be acting a dishonourable part to remain—unless with your permission. Do you understand me now?"

He asked his question in a low, eager voice, gazing intently into her downcast, blushing face. She did not reply at once; but when he repeated his question, she said, in as low a tone as his own,

"I scarcely think that I do."

"Tell me to go away, then—that you will be glad to see me depart!"

"No—I cannot say that," she replied. Then she went still more rapidly towards the house, and he did not seek to follow her. On the contrary, he went back to the verge of the cliff, and looked out to sea again, and down at the shingle below him, whence he had climbed, one stormy night, towards the light which guided him to Abel Wrayford's study. Towards the greater light which seemed now, to his sanguine fancy, to be guiding him towards the English girl whom, in his weeks of forced idleness, he had learned to love. He could not own that passion to the guardian yet awhile, for he was penniless, and the confession would only render him an object of suspicion; he would not confess it to her until he was sure of her affection, till he read in her manner, in her look, a something more than a wish that he should not leave her guardian's service. He took hope to his heart from that day—he believed in his future, and he almost forgot his political faith. Presently he went into the house in search of Abel Wrayford, and found that gentleman in the topmost room—a room which Abel Wrayford's father, a man of studious frame of mind, had persuaded his landlord to build for him on the leads of the house—deep in his chemicals, measuring his acids with a steady hand, and counting every drop which fell from the vial into the saucer he held beneath it.

"I have come to ask you, Mr. Wrayford," he said, "to allow me to change my intention."

"Intention! What intention?" said Wrayford, absently.

"Of going away this afternoon. I should like to remain, and be of use to you, if I can."

"All right. I am glad to hear that you are not foolhardy, and going away in search of a start in London is foolhardiness in these times, Victor. What colour is that?"

He passed the saucer to Victor, who scrutinized it, and could make nothing of it.

"It's a dirty kind of blue, I think," said Victor, after a moment's reflection.

"Exactly," he replied. "That is the second time that I have been pottering up here in search of a colour that has no existence, save in my wool-gathering brains."

He took the saucer from the young Frenchman's hand, and flung it and its contents into the fire which was burning there—flung it with great gravity and determination, and with no evidence of anger in his thoughtful face.

"So an end to the last new craze, and a beginning to sober work, Victor Dufoy," he said.

CHAPTER IV.

ROBERT TRUSTWORTH, MASTER-FISHERMAN.

ABEL WRAYFORD was a man as good as his word; he worked hard after that day, wrote early and late, kept to the practical part of his profession, allowed no new ideas to cross his mind, or, at all events, to disturb it, and succeeded in having his quarter's rent ready the day before Mr. Trustworth called for it. Mr. Robert Trustworth, master-fisherman, it may be said here, was an odd man in his way, and in everybody else's way, and it did not surprise Abel Wrayford that he took his cash without a "Thank you," and tied the string round the throat of his money-bag with a savage jerk, as though he were rather disappointed at finding his rent ready.

Mr. Trustworth was not an amiable man —had never been amiable within the knowledge of the oldest inhabitant of Greymoor. Old folk in the place remembered him as the surliest young man who had ever served his time on a fishing-smack, and told strange stories of his fierceness and hardness, and doubted, more than one of them, how Robert Trustworth had contrived to earn money enough to set up in business for himself, have a ship of his own, and purchase a little house property about his native place. There were ugly whispers concerning the money that had been made from wrecking in that part of Cornwall; cruel stories of false lights luring confiding craft to the rocks, and cargoes mysteriously disappearing before the morning showed the wreck upon the coast; and Robert Trustworth, in his youth, was sup-

posed to have made his penny from this
noble little game—only supposed, for no
one had any proof to bring against his character; and when he married, and settled
down in life—shortly afterwards settling his
wife by hard words and harder treatment,
spiteful people said again—he was always
ready to explain how he had saved his
money, even to launch into details concerning the process, being a trifle boastful at
most times and seasons.

He had earned his money by speculating,
he said—by taking shares in public companies when they were starting fresh. London, and friends of his in London, gave him
private information as to which were good
and which were bad. He made no secret
of how he had got on in life, bought his
own ship, his nets, his house property—it
was only common sense, not education, fine
manners, or anything of that sort. He had
been known even to draw a comparison at
times between himself and that old Wray-

ford, although old Wrayford was four or five years his junior.

" Look at that old man with his eddica-tion, and his shutting hisself up in the house on the hill away from everybody, and his airs and graces, and dodges and ideas, that never come to anything but grief; and then look at me, sound and prosperous, and say who's got on best in the world !" he would say at times, as if Abel Wrayford preyed upon his mind, or the airs and graces to which he had referred had at one time or another jarred upon his susceptibilities. Be this as it may, certain it was that he did not like Abel Wrayford, and even envied him the good name in the village and the respect which his contemporaries paid him ; and certain it was, also, that, as dislike breeds dislike, so Abel Wrayford did not love Robert Trustworth, or admire that kind of plain-speaking which Trustworth called his frankness, and Wrayford, in ex-cited moments, his infernal impudence.

Therefore, after the rent was paid that morning, Mr. Wrayford seemed waiting a little anxiously for the pleasure of wishing Mr. Robert Trustworth a good afternoon. But Robert Trustworth was not disposed, upon that particular afternoon, to depart upon his way; he sat with his back to the window, taking up with his broad, burly form all the light which Mr. Wrayford wanted for himself, and staring stolidly at the chemist.

"You're doing pretty well, I s'pose?" he said at last.

"Yes, pretty well," was the laconic answer.

"Anything new?"

"Nothing new," was the reply.

"Ah!"

Mr. Wrayford fidgeted with the papers on his desk, and made no attempt to lead the conversation. Trustworth continued to stare in a very extraordinary manner at his tenant.

"How's Grace?" he jerked forth suddenly.

"Who?" inquired Abel.

"Grace Edmonds—your ward as is—you know."

"Oh, she is pretty well, thank you."

Mr. Wrayford knit his brows a little as he replied. He did not relish the allusion, or the friendly manner in which Trustworth had mentioned his ward's name.

"And that furrin chap—is he about still?"

"Yes. He is my assistant."

"Ah! so I've heard," said Trustworth, carelessly. "I s'pose you look after him and her a bit?"

"What the devil do you mean by that!"

Wrayford lost his temper at this last question of the master-fisherman, and showed that he lost his temper, too, by the strange, sharp expression of his features. He felt himself insulted, and he was quick

E 2

to betray the disagreeable impression which
Trustworth had created.

"I should, if I was in your place. As a
dooty—and a doubt. Them French chaps
are allers full of their monkey tricks, you
know."

"I don't know."

"He's young, and she's young; and,
though she ought to look above him, still
there's no telling what is likely to get into a
woman's head. But she's a nice gal, mind
you."

"Do you mind getting a little more out
of the light?" asked Abel Wrayford, setting
himself to his desk. "I am pressed for
time to-night, Mr. Trustworth, and have a
long paper to finish."

"I shan't keep you much longer. Look
'ee here."

Wrayford looked at his tormentor, who
had suddenly begun to clench his fist, and
to hammer at the broad, horny palm of his
left hand.

"Well, I'm looking."

"I don't think any harm of your ward, and lots of what's good."

"Is it any particular business of yours?"

"Yes, for I'm interested in her."

"Thank you," answered Wrayford.

"Interested in her more than you thinks, old man."

"Confo——go on! What have you to say, Robert Trustworth, that you worry me like this?" cried Wrayford. "Has anything happened?—have you any bad news for me?"

"Bad news!—no, I ain't."

"Then, for heaven's sake, get away to your fish, and leave me to my work!"

"I ain't got no fish to go to," said Trustworth, surlily, "till I sails out with the moon to-night. I want to talk to you about your ward. I likes her."

"Eh?"

"I say I likes her," shouted Trustworth; "I spose that's English, and you're not any

deafer than usual, Wrayford. Oh! she
knows it well enough, and you ought to
know it too, if you had any eyes for anything save that silly work of yourn. I've
liked her from a child; and as she's growed
and growed, so I've said and said to myself,
'If ever that gal gets to be a woman, and
goes on well, I'll make her a good offer.'
It's been a kind of waiting of her that
I have been, Wrayford — there, that's
frank."

Wrayford had just breath enough to gasp
out,

"Yes, it's frank—damned frank!"

"You know my position in this place,"
he continued—"what I am, what I have
come to by my henergy. This house I
bought when old Selwyn died, you know,
and that there row down by the little jetty in
the village; and my shop's my own, and three
hundred pound worth of nets; and there
ain't a mortgage nowhere. I'm as good a
man—I daresay a better man—than anyone

in Greymoor, and a catch for any woman. It's a chance for Grace—she's young, but I'm ony two-and-forty myself, Wrayford, and full of health and sperits. It mayn't strike her at fust, but she will get used to the notion, for it's a good chance, that lots of gals would jump at. Why, the widder at the 'Lobster Inn' has been a-jumping at it ever since I buried Mrs. T——."

Wrayford had ceased to pay any attention to this self-eulogium. He had made a savage dash at the ink, and commenced writing; and, to Robert Trustworth's fancy, it seemed as if the student were taking down in black and white all those qualifications on which he had waxed eloquent. But Wrayford was trying to write him down, to forget that this obnoxious individual had obtruded into his presence; and although the effort was an impossibility, he contrived to write with great rapidity sentence after sentence, of a vague and incomprehensible character. When there was a pause, Wrayford looked

up at the big, evil-looking man by the.
window.

"You wish to marry my Grace?"

"Well, I don't think you can make a
mistake there."

"When she has given you her consent to
the match, you can call for mine.   Good
afternoon."

"Then you've no objection?"

"Man, I will tell you my objection afterwards, if it ever come to mine.   If Grace
give you her answer, a flat and decisive
No, there will not be any occasion for us to
talk of this again."

"Oh! yes, there will."

"I tell you there will not!" cried Wrayford, with more fierceness, and bringing his
hand smartly down upon the desk; "can
you not see that?"

"Blest if I can!   You don't mean to
say——"

"I say nothing more, Robert Trustworth.
I would rather not speak out all that is in

my thoughts at present—I am too excited.
I have work to do, and wish to keep calm."

" Yes; bu——"

" I think I did say good afternoon ?"

" Oh ! good afternoon to you. It's never
not much good a-talking to you, Wrayford ;
but you'll think over all that I've said to
you after I am gone."

He departed, very much like a man who
had been treated unceremoniously ; and he
slammed the door noisily behind him. He
went away cursing Abel Wrayford's want of
ceremony. He was a rich man, and had
made a noble offer, of which the silly
chemist did not see all the advantages at
present. In good time he would, no doubt.
He marched down the hill from the lonely
house as if all Greymoor belonged to him ;
and Abel, who had left his desk, watched him
along the sloping path towards the village.

" He will meet Grace," he muttered to
himself, " and frighten the poor girl with
his outrageous love-making. What an odd

idiot he is, to be sure! What a mad fancy
to get into his ugly head!"

He sat down by the window in the full
glare of the afternoon sun, which came in
upon him there, and thought, of all the
oddities and inconsistencies of life, this was
the oddest and the strangest. An old man
like Trustworth—not very old perhaps, not
old at all, in fact, scarcely middle-aged!—but
an illiterate, ill-mannered, ugly, and bad-
tempered fisherman, to insult him by a proposal for the hand of Grace Edmonds!

"I should not have dreamed of that man
thinking of my ward," he said; and then
words which Robert Trustworth had spoken
in the room rang so forcibly in his ear that
he muttered them aloud. He sat down by
the window at last, and reflected deeply, reflected himself into a bad temper, and
stamped upon the floor in his new rage.
"To think that I should be disturbed by
anything that that unlicked bear could say
to me!" he cried, getting up from the

window at last, and beginning to pace the room to and fro in a bear-like fashion himself. How long he promenaded in that manner he never knew; the sunlight faded from the room and from the sea, the twilight was upon him, and he was still forgetful of his work, when a voice, full of the music that he loved best, brought him back to waking life.

" Why, Gardy, what is the matter?"

He looked round. Grace was standing in the room, taking off her bonnet and shawl, and regarding him with anxiety.

" Nothing is the matter, my dear—that is, not much the matter. I have been put out a little."

" Has another idea failed?"

" Oh! no."

" And you have not let another craze take possession of you, or been carried off by that old colour project, which was quite ten pounds out of our way, Gardy?"

" No. I have been put out of temper by

a visitor. But I will tell you all over our tea. Where's Victor?"

"Why, have you not sent him to Penzance?"

"Yes, so I have," he said absently; "and we shall have a quiet tea together, as in the old times before he came."

"Yes—father and daughter alone once more."

"To be sure," he added, slowly, and after a long pause.

Grace regarded him with great attention, but did not press him with any anxious questions. She would leave him to confess what had disturbed him presently. She saw that he was very different from his usual self, and entrenching on a deeper line of thought, which cast its shadow on a face that had a habit of betraying anything that disturbed its owner. He looked very strange that afternoon—as if a great sorrow, a great disappointment were weighing him down. She could almost fancy that his dear patient

face had become more lined, and his hair a
streak or two more grey since she had gone
marketing to Greymoor. She should be
glad to listen to all that had disturbed his
equanimity, and then she would tell him
something in return, to bring the smiles back
to him.

When they were taking tea together, and
she was sitting opposite, the fairest and best
of tea-makers, he said,

" Did you meet anybody this afternoon ?"

" Yes, I seemed to meet everybody in
Greymoor."

" Did you meet Mr. Trustworth ?"

" To be sure !   And what do you think ?"
she cried, laughing very pleasantly, and
clapping her hands together as she spoke—
" what *do* you really think that he said to
me ?"

" I think that I can guess. He asked
you to marry him."

" Why, who told you ?"

" He came here first of all with his proposition, Grace, and I referred him to you, knowing what answer he was sure to re‐ ceive."

"Then it is he who has been troubling you?"

"I suppose I must say it is," replied Wray‐ ford; "and yet what was there to trouble myself about, after all? What did you say to him?"

"That I was very much flattered by his preference, but that I had no thought of marrying at present; and I hinted, as delicate‐ ly as I could, to a man who requires strong hints to impress him—that under any cir‐ cumstances it was not probable that I should marry Robert Trustworth."

"What did he say, Grace?"

"He was very much offended, but he told me that I should think better of it."

Guardian and ward both laughed at this —the guardian rubbing his hands together in his excitement.

"There's an end to poor Trustworth's

dreaming," he said; "and I feel for the man in my way, for I think he was sure of you, and thought it impossible that so influential a being in the parish should be so summarily set on one side. I daresay he has his feelings, Grace, and will be very sorry in his way—in his own heart, as it were."

"Why should he be sorry?" asked Grace.

"He has built his hopes on you—he said this afternoon that he had been waiting for you, that he had been watching you grow up to womanhood,—waiting and watching thus, and hoping year by year that you would keep good and turn to him at last."

"Why, Guardian—is this really you?" she cried.

"Really myself. Why not?" he asked.

"You are arguing in defence of one whom I am sure you dislike," she said, "and pleading his cause, as if you thought it would be a good thing for me to marry that cross, evil-looking man."

" No, no, I don't think that," he said hur-
riedly. " What was I saying? God bless me,
child, I would not have you marry him for
the world!"

" Robert Trustworth of all men," she cried,
a little indignantly, " who has not spoken to
me twenty times in his life, and has always
been cruel and hard—who never gave a
kind word to a living soul, and at whose
past life and deeds men shake their heads
and whisper to each other. The idea is a
horror to me."

" Quite right. It is a horror to me."

" And yet——"

" And yet I am thinking of his disappointment. True—forgetting that he was a man
not likely to grieve. Not a man who has
understood you, known your worth, seen
you grow up day by day under his own eyes,
a bright loveable thing for the heart to
cherish, and pray and hope for, as some
good folk here and there pray for heaven,
Grace."

"No—his was not a love like that," she answered very thoughtfully.

He glanced eagerly across the table at her, and she looked across and smiled at him. What a load that smile took from his aching heart!

"Still we will not make fun of Trusty Rob, as I have heard Trustworth called before this," said Wrayford; "no man asks a woman to marry him without some respect in his heart towards her—and he has riches, Grace."

"Yes—he is rich."

"My theory is that no man has a right to ask a woman to become his wife, unless he has paved the way, by caution and forethought, to a comfortable home for her. If he can offer that, if he is sure of her future and his own, then he has a right to speak out—not else."

"I believe that," said Grace warmly.

Was she thinking of Victor Dufoy at that moment, when her cheeks crimsoned, and

her eyes sought the ground ?—was she content to wait for Victor to speak, feeling assured that, when his future showed a promise, or gave forth a hope, he would tell
her of his love ?

"You believe that a man should be silent
until the path ahead of him is free from
difficulty ?"

" Yes."

" It would be possible for you, Grace—
for you are a woman who should think a
little of all this, and expect to be troubled
by a suitor now and then—to wait for such
a man, confident in his love for you, and in
that honour which keeps him silent till the
better times ?"

" I would wait all my life for such a man."

" And yet position is difficult to attain,
and the man in striving for it may grow
grey and old," said Wrayford.

" Keeping his heart young for my sake,
though, and not turning from one getting
old along with him."

She spread her hands before her face,
and cried a little to herself—for it was rather
a miserable picture, for all its romance, that
she had conjured up; and a grey-haired
couple, sundered by want of means, was
not a cheering, soul-sustaining object. She
was startled by her guardian's hand upon
her shoulder.

"Courage, Grace; we may be nearer
than you think."

He went away at once to his study on
the topmost floor, and Grace did not remind
him that it would be better to write on
steadily that evening than begin—as he was
sure to begin up there—his wild and useless
experiments. That work of stability was
her guardian's worst foible; if he had been
less full of crotchets, less clever, perhaps,
he would have been a wealthier man.

She did not call him back. She wanted time to think of that which he had
said to her—the kind, cheering words
which had stirred her heart, and had im-

plied that he had guessed a great deal of all that that heart contained. He was thinking of poor Victor's poverty, of Victor's hopes of recovering his property some day, and returning to them rich ; he had seen, with his usual perspicacity, that, silent and reserved as Victor was—as he was bound in honour to be—and silent and reserved as she was herself, they were waiting in their hearts for one another. What a girl's romance it was! This good second-father had read the story clearly—perhaps more clearly than Victor Dufoy had—and, with his natural gentleness and generosity, had told her of his knowledge, in his own kind way. It was like him—it was like his great deep thoughts of her.

And Abel Wrayford, in his study, where no experiments were attempted that night, was thinking of his ward, and pacing the room in the old wild-beast fashion which Grace had interrupted downstairs. He looked a younger man by many years that night; his face was bright and hopeful; his eyes were full of light; he flung his head back proudly as he walked, and stooped no longer forwards with the burden of his thoughts. There was a thought which had given new life to him, and strengthened the hope of many a year.

"She understands me at last—she believes in me, and will wait," he murmured.

CHAPTER V.

THE GREAT SUCCESS.

AFTER that night there set in a run of
ill-luck to Abel Wrayford's home—
ill-luck so persistent and heavy that many
men with less faith in the future or in themselves would have given way beneath it.
Strange to relate, it did not affect for the
worse the spirits of the chemist of Greymoor ; on the contrary, they seemed to rise
at every disappointment, and no one was more
smiling or bright than he who found the world
suddenly shutting its gates against him, and
leaving him without the walls which kept
prosperity away. The *Scientific Register*, a
paper on which Abel Wrayford had worked

for years, died for want of patronage, after
being gradually extinguished by the light of
a showier and shallower contemporary. Abel
Wrayford suffered with the rest, and lost
much labour which had been pleasant and
profitable to him ; but he was not dispirited.
His old publisher, sitting complacently in
the shadow of the Bankruptcy Court, wrote
to him encouraging letters, and talked of
starting afresh when he was free; and Abel
waited for the better times along with him.

"The long lane must have a turning,
Grace," he said, when she looked duller and
sadder than her wont. "You must have
confidence with me."

Grace tried very hard to have confidence ;
but it did not bring any ready-money
into the house, or stop running further and
further into debt at the little tradesmen's
shops lying at the hill's foot. Rent day
arrived, the bleak Lady-day quarter, and
there was Robert Trustworth to face, and to
ask for a little delay, as times had been bad

with them. Wrayford asked the favour,
not Grace, when the big man came for his
money.   He asked for it calmly and re-
spectfully, as befitted a tenant who was, as
Trustworth phrased it afterwards, "down on
his luck," but with a dignity which told not
of any great humility of spirit.   Abel Wrayford considered that he had a right to ask
this favour, he and his father having lived
in that house for half a century at least;
but, as Robert Trustworth had only recently
bought the property, he did not see the matter quite in the same light, and said so.

"You will understand that I can pay this
rent by the sale of a few books and my
chemical apparatus," said Wrayford, " and
that must be done if you are anxious for
your money.   I am in your hands."

Robert Trustworth considered the position
for awhile.

"Well, I'll let it stand," he said at last.
" It doesn't matter to me, a few pounds.
I've a good income.   Why, some shares I

bought last year in the Joint Stock Amalgamated Company sent me down fourteen per cent. last week."

"I congratulate you."

"Thank'ee."

He went from the house without asking how Grace Edmonds was, or without mentioning her name, and he swaggered home with his hands in his pockets, which were lacking in their rights as to Abel Wrayford's rent. Wrayford thought that he had forgotten the rejection of his suit, and had outlived any disappointment, like a sensible and hard-headed man. But Wrayford had formed a wrong conception of Robert Trustworth's character. Trustworth was dogged and secretive. He had taken a fancy to Grace Edmonds, in much the same way, perhaps, as a dog-fancier might take a liking for some lovely specimen of a King Charles's spaniel, and he was "set on her" none the less for the rejection of his suit. She was pretty, young, and to his taste. "The

old gal," as he always called the preceding
Mrs. Trustworth, was hot-tempered, old, and
plain as he was. He had spent a great deal
of his life in knocking her about, but he was
sure that he should pet and spoil this darling.
He could not get her out of his thoughts,
or think of anybody else, although there
were heaps of better matches in a pecuniary
sense. He had resolved to try a different
tack, and go in for amicability and general
kindness to everybody; and he was glad in
his heart when he found that Abel Wrayford was back in his rent. Grace would
think it kind of him to allow the rent to
fall into arrear; and, by Heaven! it should
go another quarter! Then, when they were
very poor, and did not know which way
to turn, he would ask Grace again to be
his wife; and if it came to No again, he
should show his teeth a little—just a little!
He was not going to be kind, and to keep
his mouth on the eternal grin for ever—it
was painful to him, for he was not used to

it. But he would hold on as long as he could—until the Midsummer quarter, that was—and then he would clear the deck for action.

When the Midsummer quarter arrived, the ill-luck of the Wrayfords was still running on as swiftly and regularly as ever. Abel Wrayford might be more thoughtful, but his spirits had not undergone abatement—he was a trifle more serious occasionally, that was all. He spoke very hopefully, though he might not exactly see his way; and Grace noticed with a sigh that he was fuller of experiment than ever, and that the light in the upstairs room— Wrayford's Nest, as it was called by the townsfolk—burned far into the night.

Things were steeped very much in shadow when the Summer weather came round, and all was brightness out of doors, and across the blue sea beyond the windows of their room. The books, and much of the chemical apparatus, had been sold quietly by

Wrayford, not to cover the rent, but to pay
poor shopkeepers who were pressing with
their claims from Greymoor. Trustworth
was a rich man, and would give them time;
the lane *was* very long, but they must be
close upon a turning.

Abel Wrayford was surprised one day—a
fortnight after quarter-day—by young Dufoy.
He was writing in the Summer-house—a
favourite haunt of his in Summer, that he
had built himself of lattice-work, over
which Grace had trained a hundred roses—
and deep in calculation, fighting his way
through an army of figures which required
grave. and earnest study, for they were
figures of quantity, and affected the life and
death of an old craze which had come suddenly upon him again in his misfortune—
like a hope that would not be set aside—
when Victor Dufoy's presence suddenly
robbed him of a little light.

"Ah, Victor!" he said, looking up,
"where have you been all the week?"

"I have been to Launceston, for one place."

"That's not attending to work," he said, beginning to trifle with his pen.

"But there was no work here ready to the hand, sir."

"Ah! that's true," replied Wrayford; "and, by the way—God bless me! there is money owing you, too, and you must live, pay for your apartments down in Greymoor, and all that, as well as other people. How forgetful I am! How much can you do with for a week or two?" And Abel felt in his pockets, and found a few half-pence there, which he jingled together dismally.

"I was not thinking of money, sir," said Victor, proudly; "I am for ever in your debt, not you in mine. But I have been thinking," he added, as his voice changed, and even faltered, "of leaving Greymoor for a time."

"Indeed! Are you thinking of *La Belle*

France, or of the cousin of whom you told me once?"

"The cousin, sir?"

"Yes, the *fiancée*—why, Victor, you have not forgotten your engagement?"

"It was not an engagement—simply a wish of my mother's; and the cousin got married some time since, against everybody's desire, save her own—and mine. I thought that I had told you."

"Not a word. Well," he said, a little testily, "where are you going?—why do you wish to go?"

"I wish to go, for the reason that I feel I am of no further use to my benefactor— rather an encumbrance."

"What makes you think that?"

Wrayford was a proud man, and had carefully concealed his difficulties from his assistant. He would have struggled on with him a little longer, trusting still to a turn in his favour, rather than have confessed that he was not able to keep him. And

now this sharp-eyed Frenchman had guessed
the secret, unless Greymoor folk had been
talking too much amongst themselves.

"I can see, sir, that affairs are not going
so straight with you as I could wish—that,
in fact, I am, for a time, a little in the way.
I am sure, if I go, it will be the better for us
all."

"Well," said Wrayford, thoughtfully,
"perhaps you are right, Victor. I thank
you for your consideration. Luck has been
dead against me lately, and until there's
a rift in the clouds to let the sunshine
through, it may be as well to part. But I
shall be sorry to lose you."

"Oh! sir, how sorry shall I be! To you
and your kind ward, I owe all the happiness
of my life."

"I don't see much happiness in working
on here. You may do better in London. I
will run over all my correspondents presently, and see if any of them are worth
giving you a letter of introduction to. I

never dreamed of your going away, Victor."

Victor shrugged his shoulders and looked disconsolate.

" When do you think of departing ?"

" This very day."

" Why, that's hasty work !"

" Now that my mind is made up, it is better to break off at once the ties which bind me here."

The ties! What was the young man raving about? thought Wrayford. Was this French sentiment at parting, or real feeling? Real feeling, probably, for he was sorry himself to lose this light-hearted, good-tempered, tolerably clever young fellow.

" At all events, do not leave us till the evening," said Wrayford, turning over his papers again. " I may have something to tell you."

Victor looked at him very eagerly.

"I may, or may not," said Wrayford, "for I am perplexed with figures this morning, and there is really something in them.

Do you remember my notion of the new colour—the new bright, heaven-sent violet of which I have dreamed? Well, I have come back to that idea, for the want of something better to do, and last night I was close upon it upstairs."

"I wish you every success, sir," said Victor, regarding his senior almost compassionately.

"Of course. For it is to your interest as well as mine," he said. "Now leave me, Victor, to struggle with an old fancy."

Victor went a few paces from him, and then returned.

"I—I should like to say a few words to Miss Grace before I go away."

Wrayford was absorbed in his studies. He did not look up, or the agitated expression of the assistant's face might have scared him.

"She has gone down to the town with some lace, which, poor girl, she hopes to sell before she comes back. You cannot fail to meet her. She will be sorry—decimal eight, ten, six—to hear of your leaving us thus suddenly."

Victor darted away, and Wrayford did not know he was gone. The chemist of Greymoor was really struggling hard with his idea, endeavouring to wrest from it a truth or a fact which might not lie within it, study how he would, and the minutes stole on that Summer afternoon without his taking heed of them. At another time the going away of Victor Dufoy would have troubled him a great deal, for he had "taken" to the foreigner; but here was an idea, gigantic, and teeming with material, and it was necessary to work hard before he dismissed it for ever—this time positively for ever—from his thoughts, or clung to it as to a promise of good fortune which should make amends for all the bad by which he had been beset.

He did not know that hours had passed by, and that Robert Trustworth had taken the place of Victor Dufoy, until his name was called out harshly. Then he looked up and saw—and an unpleasant sight it is to a man back in his rent—his landlord standing before him.

"Good afternoon, Mr. Trustworth. For heaven's sake, man, keep quiet for a moment!"

"What for? What's the matter?" asked Trustworth.

"I am half-way—three-quarters of the way—towards a discovery, if figures stand . for anything. Figures denote quantities, and I think I see my way."

"I wish you saw your way to making my rent square, Wrayford—that would be a mightier pretty prospect."

"It shall be all right in time. Do not interrupt me at this minute, there's a good fellow."

"But I ain't a good fellow!" cried Trustworth—"I ain't a-going to be a good fellow no longer."

" Eh ?—what has happened now ?"

Abel Wrayford glanced at him half carelessly, observed that it was a dark and
lowering face which he encountered, but
he was only half interested. The spell of the
figures was on him, and he could not break
away from it.

" I saw your proud peacock ward this
afternoon, and I told her my mind, after
she was too high and mighty to be common
civil to me.   I made her another offer this
afternoon, and was treated wus than ever.
Now that won't do."

" How foolish of you to subject yourself
to a second refusal !" said Wrayford—" to
dash head-first at an insurmountability, as
this is. You should have known—you must
have seen that Grace is not a girl to change
her mind."

" I've done with her—I've guv her up !"
cried Trustworth, passionately. " I ain't
lived all these years for nothing, to be jilted
and down-trodden by a chemical minx! I'll

have her know, and you know—you know, Abel Wrayford," he shouted, bringing his great dark hand down upon the desk, and surprising the student at it, "that I'm not a man who's a-going to be trifled with. If I was poor, and as desperate as I have been, I'd have her off in my ship one night, and nobody should hear of her again."

"Eh! the devil you would!"

"But I have a stake in the place, a name to keep up, and 'ouses to hold on by, and she can go, and that for her!" he cried, snapping his fingers in the air.

"That's a sensible way of putting it," said Wrayford, his eyes turning again wistfully towards the long rows of figures before him. The spell was very strong upon him then, for Trustworth might have been a dream-figure, after the first signs of passion had exhibited themselves. He was conscious that Trustworth was abusing him and his ward, demanding his rent, and threatening

a distress-warrant; he was even certain that
the master-fisherman had sworn a big oath
that there should be brokers in the house
before twenty-four hours had passed, but
he was dreaming on still, and trying to
check the torrent of rage by absent little
monosyllables.

Suddenly he woke up to life, and startled
his irate landlord. He rose to his feet with
a precipitancy that would have alarmed
most people, he upset his desk on the
gravel, and glared before him with his two
hands, full of papers, shaking violently:

" Ha !—I see it !"

"See it!—see what?" cried Trustworth,
taken off his guard, and turning round and
round—" is it anything alive?"

" I see it all—all which has so long
baffled me—and there is fortune—glorious
fortune, within a stone's throw! The new
colour, man, is mine—I'm sure of it! I'll
call it Wrayfordine; I'll—don't stop me;

don't stand in my way; let me get up to The Nest."

He rushed past Robert Trustworth, and along the garden path, into the house, tossing his arms wildly in the air, and heeding not his broken desk, and the chaos which had followed its disruption. Trustworth looked after him, and rubbed his temples vigorously.

"He's quite mad. His troubles have done it at last, and serve him right too! He's as mad as his ward, who doesn't know what a chance she has lost—the stuck-up chit!"

Meanwhile Abel Wrayford was in his study, mixing, compounding, bustling about with nervous hands, running to and fro from the furnace to several glass saucers upon the table, tilting the contents of one into another, measuring off certain liquids into phials with accuracy, despite his shaking hands, finally finishing his labours with a yell of triumph which it was as well that his friends did not hear.

" Successful !—successful at last !" he cried. " It will bring—it must bring a fortune to Grace and me. The new colour is a fact—born of heaven, one of heaven's gifts to me this lucky day !"

An odd man was Abel Wrayford ; for he was a thankful one. Few philosophers would have knelt down and thanked God for the discovery; but he did, before he repaired to his parlour more composed, although very nervous still, to communicate the glad tidings unto Grace. She was not in the parlour, but she was advancing to him, though his eyes had not seen her from the window yet. She was close upon him, and Victor Dufoy was by her side, his arm round her waist, his handsome face looking down into hers, as his lips discoursed the eloquence of love ; of a passion which had o'ermastered prudence, and leaped over all conventionalities in the agony of the parting which was close upon them.

They were coming on together, full of

love for, and of trust in one another, forgetful, perhaps, of all the world besides themselves —even of Abel Wrayford waiting for their coming.

The chemist of Greymoor saw them finally, and the light which had lingered on his face suddenly and strangely died away. There were papers in his hands, but they fluttered from his grasp to the ground, and the hands wandered restlessly to his heart, to his neckcloth, which he loosened, as though a sense of suffocation was creeping upon him, to which he must succumb. The old triumphant words hovered on his lips still, but with a bitter, sarcastic meaning, which was the whisper of a terrible despair:

"Successful!—successful at last!"

CHAPTER VI.

DISAPPOINTMENT.

WHEN Victor had left Abel Wrayford, after broaching the subject of his departure from Greymoor, he had gone slowly down the steep path towards the village, in search of Grace. The chemist had told him that his ward was to be found in that direction—a superfluous piece of information, however, he having accompanied Grace some distance on her journey at an earlier period of the day. Grace and he had had a long and serious conversation together that morning, and the result had been Victor's suggestion to Abel, as we have detailed in our preceding chapter. The result of his interview with Abel Wrayford was now to be communicated to Grace, and when he was within a stone's throw of the village, he sat down on a grassy slope to wait for her.

There was a fair prospect before him, but it did not cheer his heart much, for he was going away that evening in great trouble and incertitude. The sea, which had cast him a wounded man upon the shore, stretched before him, fair, smiling, and deceptive; the peaceful village was at his feet; above him on the rocks was perched the old picturesque house which had been his home, and where he had spent his happiest days; and the bright cloudless sky was over all. Gazing mournfully towards the house in the distance, he fancied that he could see the dim figure of the student pass and repass the window of his "Nest," and he shrugged his shoulders, as if in pity for the last craze which had taken Abel from honest work and sober care for his ward.

He waited long and patiently for Grace Edmonds, thinking of his future, and wondering if, in the far distance, hers would cross it, and flood his life with light. The sun sank lower in the sky—it was almost time to think of going away, and still he sat there dreaming. Only one man passed him whilst he waited, for there was no cross cut to a second village above him, but a round-about and dangerous cliff-path, which no one followed, save an adventurous tourist or artist occasionally, in the long Summer days which were upon them.

Honest Robert Trustworth had marched by in hot haste, with his iron-looking hat pulled over his brows; but Victor had not noticed him, so deeply were his thoughts engrossing him. Trustworth had scowled at Victor, and gone on to Wrayford's house, had returned, and rewarded him with a second scowl, blacker than the first; but the dark looks of the master-fisherman had been lost upon the Frenchman. Victor was waiting for Grace—thinking only of Grace, who came at last towards him, looking almost as grave and thoughtful as he, until aware of his presence.

"Oh! Mr. Victor," she said, as she came up with him, "have you been waiting for me?"

"Yes, I have been waiting," he repeated, sadly.

She cast a quick, shy glance in his direction as the words escaped him, and the doleful ring of them suggested all the truth.

"You have told him, then?—he does not suspect that I——"

He interrupted her hastily.

"That you have asked me to leave Cornwall, and have told me of his trouble," he said—"no, he gives me credit for having discovered that myself. As if I could have believed in his masking his distress so well, or had eyes for anything save—save my own selfishness," he added, after a short

pause, during which Grace looked down and
crimsoned very much.

They went slowly together along the upward path, both silent for awhile. Victor
was the first to speak.

" I am going away to-night," he said, with
a suddenness that startled her.

"To-night !" she exclaimed, in her surprise. " Is there—is there any occasion for
this precipitation ?"

" Yes—he is poor," he answered.

" But——"

" And I feel that I have, in my ignorance
—my blindness," he cried, passionately,
" added so much to his poverty by my presence that I cannot go away too soon."

" Have you told him that?"

" Yes, and he was not greatly astonished.
I think in my heart that it was a relief to
him, and saved his pride a little."

" When—when shall we see you again ?"
she asked faintly. " You will return to
France, and forget us."

"Is forgetfulness possible? Oh! Grace," he said, more passionately still, "I think you know that that is beyond me, though I have said nothing—though my honour has kept me silent until now—though I have tried very hard, if very vainly, to hide my secret in my own breast. But there are times when one must speak out, and this is one of them."

"Oh! say nothing to me now!" she said, imploringly—"no matter what is in your thoughts, remember that my dear old Abel is in trouble, and that I am troubled also."

"He has given me permission to speak to you, Grace, before I go away."

"Indeed!"

Her cheeks flushed, and she veiled her blue eyes from him once more, after a little wondering stare into his face. Her heart beat very rapidly with suspense, even with joy; for she, and this handsome young Frenchman by her side, had been thrown so much together that he had become the

hero of her little world, and in her heart
she was assured that there was no one like
her Victor. Still she did not betray her
pleasure, only her confusion a little, aud
she said, a moment afterwards, with great
innocence of expression—

"But what can you possibly want to say
to me?"

"Ah! Grace, I hope you know," he cried
—"I hope that you have seen how much I
love you."

"Oh, dear!"

"And loving you with all my heart,
you can judge what I suffer in going from
you—how I am torn by necessity from
that happiness in seeing you, and in being
near you, which has been mine so long.
Oh! dear Grace, you will give me a hope
to take away with me, to keep my heart
light in those days ahead which your presence will not brighten."

Grace was crying now, but there was
much happiness mingled with her tears,

despite her words, even her half-reproaches, which escaped her, and yet which told of his affection being reciprocated.

" But the days ahead of us lie steeped in so much shadow, Victor, it seems mockery to speak of happiness."

" I do not seek to bind you by an engagement—that would be dishonourable of a poor man, Grace," he said, " and you will give me credit for not acting impulsively in this.   But I am going away, and would take one hope with me."

" And that hope ?" she asked softly.

" Is of your waiting for me for a little while—of giving me time to strive to gain a position for myself, here or abroad—of returning a short while hence, and finding you free, and glad to welcome me to the old home.   Grace, dare I hope as much as that, or have I acted cruelly in speaking of my love at all ?   Pray answer me."

" Oh ! Victor," she murmured, "I will hope with you."

" My own dear Grace !"

Thus the day of parting was to Victor
Dufoy, in that first episode of bliss, a day
for great rejoicing. He had won her love,
she had confessed her wish to wait for him,
to believe with him in the better times of
which he had prophesied. For a few brief
moments—brief as measured by the hour-
glass, but strengthening many a struggle in the future—they forgot all but
themselves. The path leading up to Wrayford's Nest was strewn with roses, and
steeped in sunshine—there were no troubles,
poverty, or disappointment in the world in
which they moved, and all the cares of
life vanished beneath their hopefulness.
They were intensely happy, proceeding side
by side along the upward path, recking not
of the jealous eyes which watched them as
they advanced, believing not in misconstruc-
tion, seeing only a hand's throw from them
the difficulties succumbing to their energy,
and, after that,—all glory !

They were speaking of their love for one another, and their courage to wait for each other, as they came beneath the porch of Abel Wrayford's house; and it was not until they had entered the sitting-room that they went back to the real. And then it was a step made slowly and reluctantly, and they did not read at once all the meaning in that haggard face before them. Victor Dufoy said, cheerfully,

"Well, Mr. Wrayford, you see that I have been fortunate enough to find her."

When Abel Wrayford's answer came, the lovers were aware of a great change in him, and yet only three words, sternly and huskily delivered, escaped his lips.

"So I perceive," he replied.

"Oh!" exclaimed Grace, quickly; but he turned to her, and raised a hand by way of entreaty not to interrupt him. She stopped and regarded him very anxiously now. He was looking very white and haggard, his neckcloth was disarranged, a strip of his collar had been torn from his throat, as though a rough hand had grasped him there, his grey hair was dishevelled, his hands were trembling with passion or nervous agitation, she was doubtful which, until he spoke again.

"Keep still, Grace," he said. "Do not interrupt me. I am in trouble to-day, and this man is in the way. Why have you not gone?" he said, turning to Victor. "Did you not say that you were going this afternoon?"

"Yes, Mr. Wrayford," replied Victor; "but not in that ungrateful haste, which would prevent my saying good-bye to you. I have something to communicate, which——"

"I will not hear you!" said Wrayford, hastily breaking in upon him.

"Not hear me, sir—not hear me?" repeated Victor in his astonishment.

"I am only anxious that you should leave this place," said Wrayford, "and never come back to me, and her!"

"Great heaven, his studies have driven him mad!" cried Victor Dufoy.

"Oh! I am sane enough," said Wrayford, bitterly; "and cessation from study has only opened my eyes to the deceit that is around me."

"Guardian!" cried Grace again.

"To his deceit, I should have said, more justly," he replied. "For he has practised his arts on both of us too well."

"Sir, I love your ward," said Victor, impetuously, "and I have attempted no disguise of my affections."

"You are an adventurer!"

"Mr. Wrayford, you know—you must know that I have acted honourably towards you both."

"It is a lie!" was the fierce answer.

"You have seen my love for Grace—guessed Grace's love for me—or we have both been dreaming!"

"I have seen only the duplicity of a man whom I saved from starvation," replied

Wrayford sternly, "and who rewards me
for my charity by seeking to gain the affections of my ward. Leave my house at
once, and God spare me from the affliction
of your presence again!"

"Dear Abel," said Grace imploringly,
"do you know that I love Victor?—that this
man whom you treat so cruelly is my affi-
anced husband?"

Abel Wrayford glared at her, and again
the doubt of his sanity crossed the minds of
his companions.

"I—I did not know it," he gasped forth;
"but I dispute it—I set aside this beggar's
claim—this poor, paltry trick to take advantage of you. You have forgotten, Grace,
your dying father's wish, as much as you
have forgotten me and yourself."

"It was his wish that I should not marry
without your consent, and I respect that
wish and you. But, Abel, your kind heart,
your generous judgment, will estimate more

fairly Victor's affection for me. This is a surprise."

" Ay, a great surprise."

" And presently——"

" Tell him to go—for God's sake, tell him to go away at once!" cried Abel, sinking into a chair. " I cannot speak to him."

" But, Mr. Wrayford," said Victor, with quiet dignity, " I must speak to you. You have addressed words to me which in more temperate moments you will regret; you have accused me of mercenary motives—of ensnaring your ward's affections, and have taunted me with the poverty which I cannot help, and with an ingratitude which I have not had. You will be sorry for this charge presently. That I love your ward better than my life is no warrant for your suspicions. She is content to wait for me, and I will not come again until I can offer her a home. I will not bind her—I have not bound her—by a promise to become

my wife. With the uncertain future lying
before me, I could not do that. But she
has faith, and will wait a little while. When
she distrusts me, from the first moment
of her doubts she is free from any claim of
mine."

"I do not affect to understand this high-
flown nonsense," Wrayford said to Grace,
"and I do not believe in it."

"Mr. Wrayford," Victor hastened to
reply, "I am very poor, but I will outlive
your want of trust in me."

"Tell him," said Wrayford between his
set teeth, as he addressed his ward again,
"that coming here to-morrow a rich and prosperous man would only make me hate him
the more intensely. That there is nothing
in the past, nothing in his future, which can
win from me anything save contempt for
the trick which has been played upon my
confidence."

"I cannot tell him that!" murmured
Grace.

" Then tell him to go."

Wrayford went out of the room in haste ; he went back to the Nest, where the bright thought had come to him of which he had been exultant, madly exultant, only a little while since.   Now, what a change !—what a long, blank misery, stretching on without a break seemed before him from that day! He had struggled hard for wealth, but it was wealth for Grace's sake ; and now approaching it, feeling that he had only to stretch forth his hand to obtain it, knowing the value to the uttermost farthing that his discovery of the colour would bring to him, he had missed the opportunity of winning her for whose prosperity he had toiled for years.   She was gone from him for ever.

It was dark night when he went downstairs again, and found Grace sitting at the table by the lamp-light, working diligently, as in the old times before the robber came. It was so like home still that he could almost hope for her, looking at the picture. She was very pale, but it was with her old smile that she glanced towards him as he entered. The rival had passed away; would the passing fancy for him, born of a girl's first romance, follow in good time? He tried to think so, for was not Victor Dufoy a villain whom he had unmasked, and whom it was possible that he should never see again?

"You are alone?" he said, on entering.

"Yes."

"That man has gone away for ever?"

"Victor has left for London," was the evasive answer. "May I speak of him now?"

"Not yet. Give me time to recover my-self—give me a week or a fortnight, Grace, to look this calmly in the face."

"Very well," said Grace, with a long sigh.

"And now let us speak of something

else—of better times, and a different estate from this. The tide has turned, and there is good luck in store for us."

Grace regarded him dubiously. Was this another phase of that eccentricity which her guardian had evinced that day?

"The colour is fixed—the problem is solved, Grace. A week hence, and we shall be rich."

"Rich!" said Grace, with a little shiver— "oh dear—rich!"

She saw Victor receding further and further from her as her guardian became prosperous—she saw riches hardening Abel Wrayford's heart, and increasing in him that strange pride which he had already exhibited. Had he made this discovery before her last interview with Victor, and was it that which had made him hard, repellent, and unjust?

"When did you discover this colour, Abel?" she asked, eagerly.

" Early this afternoon."

" I knew it—I was sure of it !" she cried. She gave way suddenly, and burst into tears, burying her face in her hands.

Wrayford realized the position at once, and accepted it. He drew himself away from her, and searched for the papers which he had dropped upon the floor in his first agony; finding them at last folded carefully on his little table in the corner where he was inclined to work at times.

" Let her think so," he muttered to himself; " perhaps it is best."

He allowed her to weep on, though every sob went to his heart, and he tried hard to sink himself in the calculations which he had worked upon the paper. But he was not happy with the proof before him of his oncoming wealth—in all his life he had not known such awful misery.

" Rich," he muttered to himself, incessantly, as though it were a talisman which

kept him strong, and threw across his loneli-
ness, his isolation, a reflex of that brightness
to which he had thought he was advancing.

CHAPTER VII.

FURTHER EXPERIMENTS.

ABEL WRAYFORD was not wrong in
the estimation of his success. He had
been a man of many failures, which he had
kept strictly to his Nest; to the world outside he had been shrewd and practical, a
safe man, for nothing of which he was
doubtful had gone out to the world. He
was sure of his colour; he knew the right
channel in which to work, and where to
make the most of his success; he was
known in London, and chemists and manu-
facturers had faith in him. The new violet
found its way speedily into public favour;
people talked of it; silken and woollen

fabrics took new hues from it; there was
that glorious proof of success which no
criticism can give, no extensive adver-
tising bestow, and only the giant impulse
of the public, following, as it were, its
instincts, can impart. Everybody talked
of Wrayfordine; and the inventor of the
colour remained in his Cornish home, un-
stirred by the murmur of the crowd. He
had sold his rights to a speculative firm,
and was content with a few thousand pounds,
and a royalty on future profits. Before the
year was out, his royalty, even to the surprise of those who had invested in the
colour, brought him some thousands more;
and Abel Wrayford woke at last to the
reality of riches.

He did not look any the better or brighter
for his triumph; he did not change out-
wardly; the good folk in Greymoor were
not aware at first that he had come suddenly into money. His habits were as quiet
and methodical as ever; the light in the Nest

burned as late into the night; he wore the same shabby vestments; and when seen in the village, or met upon the cliff, he had the same thoughtful, far-away look which " Old Wrayford " always had.

Robert Trustworth, master-fisherman, was the first to suspect that there had come a change to Abel Wrayford's home. He put the broker in for two quarters' rent, as he had threatened; he was building on the humiliation of Grace, and her prayers to him for mercy, which he would refuse contemptuously; he was laughing quietly to himself at Abel Wrayford's bewilderment and rage, when the broker came to say that the money was paid in full of all demands, and that Mr. Wrayford would be obliged by a receipt. Trustworth thought that Abel Wrayford had made a great sacrifice of his cherished instruments to pay the money, until weeks afterwards, when he found Abel bidding briskly against him for a piece of ground adjacent to the Nest, which had been put up for auction. Abel secured the ground, and Trustworth felt suddenly that he was no longer the greatest man in Greymoor.

"That old man has been and stole something," he said, with an oath, as he marched out of the coffee-room of the hotel where the auction had taken place. And by degrees it reached even Greymoor that Abel Wrayford had stolen something—stolen a secret from Nature, and made his fortune by the theft.

Time went on; the Summer gave place to Autumn, and there were brown leaves eddying about the Cornish lanes; Autumn succumbed to Winter, and to a fierce Winter, which brought rough seas and keen winds to this western point of England. Abel clung to his home still, and his ward kept house for him, as in the old days, when he was poor. His first impulse had been to quit Cornwall, to launch forth, to take Grace abroad, and seek society with her, but he

shrank suddenly from his project, and Grace
was glad of his change of intention. Abroad
they might meet Victor Dufoy, he thought,
and he had a hope in his heart that she was
learning to forget him, that it had been a
passing fancy, which time would destroy, if
he took no heed of it. He had never
talked with Grace upon the subject from
that strange day of his disappointment,
when the fulfilment of one hope was check-
mated by the loss of another; he had told
her, when they were verging upon the subject
once, that it would be merciful to him not
to speak of Victor; that there was no reasoning of hers could alter his opinion that
Victor had taken an ungenerous advantage
of his position, and that, foiled in his schemes,
he had disappeared for ever. As time
went on, and no letter came from the hand
of him who had spoken of his love, Abel
watched furtively for the signs of her distrust appearing with his own. They would
come in time; Grace would not cling al-

ways to the false—it was not in her nature;
and when she owned to him that the scales
had fallen from her eyes, he would tell all
the truth at which she had never guessed.
Meanwhile, he was content to wait, although
in waiting he knew that he had changed a
great deal, and become a stern, hard man.
People in Greymoor· said that his prosperity had made him very proud, and
thought that it was natural, and that they
would have been as proud as he with only
half his money; but at that period he was
never more humble in his heart, and never
more unhappy. For though it was pleasant
to him, almost consolatory, to talk of hope,
there were many chances against him; he
was growing older and greyer every day,
and there might be truth and honour in the
Frenchman, and defiance to him who sought
to sunder them.

In the early Spring, London was shaken
by one of its panics—the money-market
was agitated to its centre, banks collapsed,

public companies shrivelled up by scores, wealthy men became beggars, and ruin seemed everywhere at once. Ruin came down to Greymoor, seized one Robert Trustworth by the throat, and cast him back to his old place. His shares in the Joint Stock Amalgamation Company, of which we have heard him boasting, were the main source of his ruin, for the Joint Stock Amalgamation broke up, and there set in an incessant call upon the shares—calls of twenty-five and fifty pounds per share, until Robert Trustworth was as grey as Abel Wrayford. The fisherman had not borne prosperity well—had not taken to it gracefully—and his downfall was not composed or philosophical. When he had lost only half his money, he took to drinking— the idiot's inevitable refuge—and was seen staggering about Greymoor at all hours of the day; and when the last blow came, in the shape of his bank breaking up, he had *delirium tremens*, and then brain-fever, and

it was rumoured that Robert Trustworth
would not live the Spring out. Still Trustworth recovered, and before the first of
June he was to be seen at the Greymoor
beer-shops very often, and to be found
idling on the beach with old companions,
whose society he had evaded in his afflu-
ence. It was a great drop, and he raved
a great deal of his losses, but the neighbours soon grew accustomed to Trustworth's new position. He appeared to have
stepped back to his first sphere, and to the
company of the rough, ragged seamen who
haunted the shore ; he kept bad hours, and
worked with a common crew at any labour
which presented itself ; he was the Bob Trustworth that many Greymoor worthies had
known a few years since. Everybody called
him Bob now, and by a strange whim he
preferred to encounter humiliation in his
native village, and shock his contemporaries
by the rapid change in him, to beginning
life afresh where he was not likely to be

recognised. Had he borne his troubles better, this might have been heroic; but as he drank hard, and grew a reckless, desperate fellow, whom honest people shunned, it was simply bravado.

Robert Trustworth had one paramount grievance in the midst of many wrongs. He cursed The Joint Stock Amalgamation Company, and the bank which had broken with his savings in it, and all the petty misfortunes which had followed in one stream upon him, and swept him into beggary, but he cursed nothing so heartily as Abel Wrayford's luck, and hated no one so persistently and well as the man who had grown rich at the very time that his own wealth had passed away. It was a strange hate, but it was a genuine and an intense one. Abel Wrayford made every allowance for it, for he had become aware of it. He considered that trouble had turned the few brains which Robert Trustworth had ever possessed, and that the man's bitter ran-

cour was a part of the malady by which
he was afflicted. Trustworth would call
after him in the village, would dog his steps
at times, and, in his drunken moods, would
assail him with reproaches for buying up his
property in Greymoor, for no other pur-
pose than to lord it over him now that
he was a poor fisherman. Abel Wrayford, at these times, would turn away wrath
by dropping a few shillings into Robert
Trustworth's hands, and the recipient would
take them as his due, and go growling away
without any thanks for the gift. As Wrayford was weak enough to bestow his alms in
this fashion, there might possibly have been
a method in Robert Trustworth's madness,
but there was no mistake, for all that, in
the hate which the ruined man bore him
who had grown successful in the world.
In the "Lobster Inn"—the landlady of which
establishment had set her cap at honest Bob
in his better days—he would drink confusion
to the sulky chemist who lived upon the

cliff, in the house of which he had robbed him, and he would spend half the evening detailing imaginary wrongs which the malice of the upstart had wreaked upon him now that he was "down." It was Trustworth's turn to have a craze, Wrayford would say drily, when rumours of these ravings reached his ears.

This was the position of affairs when Summer came upon them, and it was twelve months since Victor had gone away. Twelve months to the very day, both Wrayford and Grace remembered, and yet neither spoke of it when they faced each other at the breakfast-table that morning. Wrayford had made up his mind to ask her if she still believed in Victor Dufoy, and he was thinking, even at that early hour, of putting this grave question to her, when the postman brought a letter to the house for Grace.

The servant laid it on the table by Grace's side, and the foreign face upon the postage-stamp told of a long distance which the missive had come in search of her, and in proof of him whom she had not learned to doubt.

" There, did I not say that he would be true ?" she cried, as though Victor had been an unceasing topic of conversation for the last twelve months.

" Who would be true ?" asked the chemist, turning very pale.

" Victor Dufoy. This letter is from Victor."

" Oh! that man !" he said, disparagingly.

The cup clattered in his saucer as he took it from the table, but Grace heeded not his excitement. She had torn open her letter, and was devouring its contents. Wrayford watched her, and saw how Grace utterly forgot him, and remembered only the man who had sent this message from his foreign home to her. The light upon her face, the sparkling of her eyes, even the sudden dimming of them by tears, and the quick heaving of her bosom, were all against him—all against

the last faint illusion which even his common
sense had not allowed him to dispel till that
day.

"Gardy," she said at last, "he is well.
He is in Italy—he will come back presently
to see us."

Abel regarded her stolidly, and she remembered that he had learned to distrust
Victor Dufoy.

"He has been a long time making up his
mind to relieve your suspense," he remarked,
coldly.

"He said, before he went away, that he
would not write until there were good news,
and words of promise for me."

"He has heard of my success," said Wrayford.

Grace would not take offence at her
guardian's remarks—she went on quickly,

"The French Government is considering
his mother's claim to the estates of which he
has spoken to us so often—there is a hope
of all being forgotten and forgiven. Oh!

Gardy, if you would only rejoice with me, how happy you would make me!"

"You forget," was the grave reproof.

"Forget what?" she asked quickly.

"That your happiness and mine are things apart, and can never be reconciled together. You will be happiest when he returns—I shall be at my worst, losing a daughter who has cheered my home, and gaining no one's confidence."

"But Victor is generous—he esteems you, and——"

"And I despise him," said Wrayford—"he will take you away without my consent——"

"Oh! you will not refuse that again, when he returns in all honour to prove his love for me?"

"When he comes back, Grace, we will speak of this. I cannot be troubled now by your romance. I have outgrown romances, child—see how grey I am!"

From that day Abel Wrayford changed

to his ward. He fostered no longer his illusion, but turned stern and cold even to her. He assumed his rightful position for the first time, accepting, before its advent, that isolation which he felt awaited him. He studied very hard, early and late, as though in the pursuit of new ideas he could forget her; and no remonstrance of her he loved could wean him from his tasks. Letters came regularly from Victor to Grace, but he asked no questions concerning them; and Grace, aggrieved at last—as what woman would not be when her lover was slighted?—did not speak of their contents to him.

Grace was very sorry for her guardian's sternness, but she felt there was no power which she possessed that could alter it or home; he had receded from her; he was no longer the kind second father who had shielded her from trouble, and studied every little wish that she had had, but a cold studious being, who wrapped himself in his pursuits away from her. One day he came downstairs earlier than was his wont, in his gloomy, prosperous latter days, and said,

" Do you visit the Lawsons as often as you used, Grace ?"

The Lawsons were the only friends in Greymoor whom Grace possessed; and about the one family in that out-of-the-way fishing-village with whom it was possible to make friends. Lieutenant Lawson had charge of a coastguard station at Greymoor, and his house was perched on the opposite hills, by the side of the little station where he held dominion. Lying between the Lawsons' house and Wrayford Nest, was the village of which we have spoken so often; and before all three was the great restless sea.

Grace looked up with surprise at the question.

" Yes, I visit them, Abel. Why do you ask ?"

"You like their company. Miss Lawson
is your own age ; the lieutenant is a gentleman, his wife a lady, and there is a certain
amount of society and cheerfulness about
their home which this does not possess. I
want you to arrange to stay with them for a
while."

"Guardian !—Abel !" she gasped forth—
"you wish this ?"

"Yes, I wish this. I am sure that it is
best. You are very much alone now—I
am compelled to leave you so often, and for
so long a time."

"Have I complained, Abel ?" she said,
reproachfully.

She was scarcely able to keep the tears
back ; he saw them in her eyes, and would
not be affected by them.

"Complained, child !—no. But I am
thinking of your happiness."

"My happiness is with you, Abel," she
replied ; "and it is strange that, after all our
years together, I should have to tell you

this, or that you cannot see it for yourself."

"Ay, it is strange," he answered, thoughtfully.

"Why have you altered like this? Is it——"

"Grace, I know what you are going to say," he said quickly; "let me ask you to dismiss that thought—that old thought—just now. You are still my daughter. I love you none the less, and if I do not think that your future happiness lies in the direction you indicate, why, leave me to my opinion, and say no more."

"But you are tired of me—I know it."

"My dear girl, I am thinking of your safety, that is all."

"Safety!"

"Yes; I have another of those crazes concerning which you used to jest once—a greater craze than all the rest, and that will make me richer than the Wrayfordine; and I think that I am as close upon the secret."

"And there is danger in your experiments?"

"Yes, a great deal of danger—I own that, Grace."

"What is this discovery, Abel?"

"A torpedo—a grand instrument for that wholesale destruction which men call war," he said—"a devilish device, which will hurl a greater number of human souls to destruction in a quicker and more certain manner than any invention of its kind that science has hitherto discovered."

"And you will make this discovery known?"

"Ay, and make myself more famous and rich than half-a-dozen paltry colours can do. Here I study glory, not beauty, Grace."

"I am sorry—I don't understand, I think."

"No ; you do not understand the value of the discovery, or what an enthusiast I have become," he replied ; "but you must understand that I cannot, for my conscience's sake, let you remain in this house twenty-four hours longer. I am constructing a gigantic specimen for government experiment, and an accident—though I am a careful man, and not likely to commit a blunder of the kind—may blow the old Nest to heaven."

Grace clasped her hands and shuddered.

"And you risk your life for this poor ambition?"

"My life is worth nothing—my ambition a great deal," he said; "my life is in my own hands—yours I have no right to risk."

"But——"

"But I have made up my mind, Grace, and for a few weeks—perhaps a few months—I must sacrifice home for the fame that, I am sure, is awaiting me. And if I sacrifice myself before the fame comes, by a mistake, what does it matter, after all?"

Grace endeavoured to persuade him from his project, insisted for a time in sharing his danger, but he was firm, and had his way at last. There was more danger to him when there were strangers in the house, he explained, than when he was alone, and careful of himself; and she went away at last, a few hours after the servant had packed her own boxes in hot haste, and fled to Greymoor with the awful news that old Mister Wrayford was turning his Nest into a powder-mill.

" I feel that we are parting as if in anger —that I shall never come back and call this home," Grace said to him.

"That is superstition."

" And you do not love me less, Abel?"

" I love you better than anyone in the world, Grace," he replied.

" And you will come and see me at the Lawsons' house ?"

" Yes—sometimes, when I am not busy, and I can leave my Robinson-Crusoe cabin here."

" And if there is any danger to you, how

am I to learn it, to be able to fly to your help, or to bring help with me, Gardy?"

Wrayford smiled at this last question.

"The danger would be past before you could reach me, child, and I should be past all the help that you could bring."

"But you might be ill, or struck down suddenly, and unable to quit the house, or let me know. No one comes up here."

"My dear Grace, your nervousness is adding every possible horror to my position. I will give you a signal from my window, when it is necessary."

Grace reminded him of his promise when he came the next week to the Lawsons, and he went away, smiling at her care for him, and yet grateful for her forethought in his heart. Her anxiety pleased him, for it showed that he had not outlived her affection yet awhile; and in his Nest, where he toiled and strove at his new work, he could fancy that her wistful looks were often

turned in the direction of his lonely home
from the house across the valley which
divided them.

CHAPTER VIII.

THE RIVAL'S RETURN.

WRAYFORD began his solitary existence with a morbid satisfaction, which
did not grow less with time. It was his
pleasure to set himself apart from his
kind, to grow more old, dogged, and un-
charitable in his "Nest." The torpedo was
his excuse to shut himself from Grace, and
to separate her from him; and though he
studied hard to perfect it, and to prepare it
for those experiments which the Government had undertaken to make—it was still
a plea behind which he concealed, almost
effectually, his desire to live alone.

He could no longer bear Grace in his home; he had given up every foolish hope that he had fostered, and had acknowledged to himself that she was too young for him, and that he had grown too old. The letters of Victor Dufoy to Grace, breathing of his affection and undying passion for her, had destroyed Abel's last chimera, and he felt that he was far too weak to hide his sorrow and his secret from one who was always at his side. It was right that she should go, and that he should remain in solitude until he had learned better to disguise himself. Grace had not dreamed of her grey-haired, sober-faced guardian loving her with all a youth's affection; and he would have preferred to die, he thought, rather than that she should guess the truth. So let him study his torpedo, until disappointment had killed him, or hardened him to stone—he cared not which. He had been away some weeks when Grace surprised him by a visit. He met her at the door with shaking hands, that would have almost thrust her back from him.

"Grace, you must never come again. This is rash of you—unfair."

"Am I in greater danger than yourself?"

"I have answered that question before," he cried, with great excitement; "and you have promised to keep away. This is a mad step. If I had made up my mind to destroy the old place, the wires might have been connected, and I hiding in safety somewhere. Who can tell?"

Grace regarded Abel Wrayford with astonishment.

"You look surprised, Grace," he said, attempting a smile, "but I have resolved upon an experiment of my own before I submit my plan to a clumsy government. Why should I not try it on the Nest?"

"Our home!"

"It is not like home now; it will never be home again to me."

"Not when I return?"

"Oh, you will not return, Grace. I am going to build a large house further inland, where the wind will swoop less at me in such bitter Winter weather as we have had lately. I am getting old, and feel the weather more acutely."

"But you will not destroy this place? This was your father's home."

"Yes," he said, carelessly, "I know that, but I have outlived my liking for it. There! leave me, and do not come again; wait for me to come to you."

"But you come so seldom. Do you know how long it is since we saw you last at Lawson's?"

"A week or two," he answered. "I will come soon—give me time."

"I have been afraid of your illness. I have been watching for your signal very often."

"You need not watch, Grace. I was never better and stronger in my life."

Grace left him puzzled by his words,

regretting the change, seeing not in the distance any brighter days in store for him. Did the pursuit of riches, the study of philosophy, render all men so hard, she wondered?

Abel Wrayford surprised Grace and her friends by a visit a few days after this, but he was not agreeable company, and Lieutenant Lawson, notwithstanding that he was an old friend, was glad when he had taken his departure. Abel was argumentative and satirical; he declined to give any details concerning the Wrayford torpedo, a topic which would have greatly interested his friend, and he entered into discussions upon naval matters, and flatly contradicted the lieutenant in every particular. He returned to his Nest in a sullen mood, and Grace shed many tears that night over her guardian's new manner.

As he went home, Abel Wrayford was met by Trustworth, who railed at him in his new abusive style, and told him, with great gravity of countenance, that he had been the ruin of him, and that it was his going up in life, which had somehow—he did not intend to explain, never mind that —cast him down. Wrayford was not so readily charitable with this forlorn wretch as usual; and Trustworth marched somewhat unsteadily by his side, talking very loudly, and followed by half-a-dozen little urchins who were out late that night, and who had become interested in the conversation.

When Wrayford had passed through Greymoor, and ascended some twenty or thirty yards of the steep path leading to the heights on which his house was built, he stopped.

" Do not come any further, Trustworth, or you may roll off the cliff when you return this way."

" I've been up here too often for that."

" Don't follow me; this is dangerous ground. They will tell you in Greymoor that I am likely at any moment to blow up the old house with my experiments."

"I know. I've heard of your last game, and the torpedo, Abel Wrayford. It's in everybody's mouth how clever you are— what a new, big fortune you are likely to make, if you don't bust yourself to bits. What right have you to grow so big, and I to be starving here?"

"Hooray!" squeaked three or four voices behind him at this question, and Trustworth turned round and made an ineffective kick or two at his *cortége*.

"I say, what right have you, and who are you, after all? You've robbed me; you've taken all my property away, and I was allers kind to you. Didn't I let you run two quarters once?—wasn't I like a brother to you allers?"

Trustworth was verging on the sentimental; he generally began with abuse, and terminated with maudlin reproaches, until Wrayford gave him money, when he launched forth into abuse again, by way of peroration. Abel began to feel for his silver at last.

" And yet nobody respects you—nobody likes you, Abel," he continued. " Your own ward keeps away from you, and is going to marry a Frenchman."

" How do you know that?" asked Wrayford, fiercely.

"Oh! I know. They talk at Lawson's, the servants do; they listen—they pick up all the news."

" Good night."

Wrayford had turned away, when Trustworth shouted after him—

" You'll give me some money—a little help, won't you ?"

" Not a farthing!" cried Wrayford— " keep sober, and earn money for yourself."

" Why——"

" And don't follow me. I am in a hasty mood to-night."

Robert Trustworth was cowed by Abel Wrayford's look; there was something new

about it which he did not admire, and which
he could not comprehend, save that it assured even his benighted faculties that the
chemist was not to be trifled with that evening. Trustworth had always set down Abel
Wrayford as a weak and feeble fellow,
and no match for a man of his size and
strength ; but there was an appearance of
toughness and ferocity about him on the
present occasion which suggested a man
who could hold his ground in conflict.
Trustworth was not a brave man at heart,
for all his bullying, and he gave in. He
did not follow Abel Wrayford to his Nest ;
he turned and ran after the little boys,
swearing fiercely in his pursuit, but failing
to catch those who had intruded on his
steps.

Abel Wrayford was seen no more for a
week, but one faithful watcher noted that
the light burned late in the topmost room,
and that the chemist's studies never seemed
to cease. He was studying hard in the

midst of his dangerous material one wild
Winter's storm, which rocked the house,
and made every timber creak in it with
ominous forebodings. On such a night as
this, he thought, as he paused now and then
to listen to the rushing of the wind and the
roaring of the angry sea, Victor Dufoy
stepped from the unknown life, and blasted
the one hope which he had had.

And on such a night Victor Dufoy came
back again, came like a spectre into the
very room where he was brooding, and
faced the man who had learned so bitterly
to despise him. He stood in the doorway
looking in upon him, his hand upon the
door, which he had opened, his dark. handsome face sad and anxious, his eyes full of
inquiry.

" Dufoy !" exclaimed Wrayford, upon
perceiving him, " what has brought you to
my house ?—how dare you come into my
laboratory unannounced in this manner?"

Abel Wrayford had recovered his surprise, and was cold and cutting as the north-east wind which rioted without.

"Your pardon for my unceremonious intrusion, Mr. Wrayford, but I knocked three times at the door. I was afraid that you were absent, or ill."

"How did you obtain admittance into the place?"

"The outer door was open."

"I must have left it unfastened, I suppose," said Abel musingly. "Well," turning sharply to his visitor, "you are here—what is it that you require?"

"I have your permission to enter, Mr. Wrayford?" he inquired.

"I have no power to forbid you the house *now*," he said, almost regretfully.

Victor Dufoy entered the room very sadly. He had come back to Greymoor full of hope, full of faith in the power of time to have cancelled an old injury, or that which Abel Wrayford had taken to himself as an injury, but his reception was a chilling one, and the young Frenchman saw at once that the difficulty before him was insurmountable.

Abel Wrayford regarded his rival with a cold but scrutinizing gaze, seeing that the world had changed with Victor, and guessing that he had brought news of his good fortune. He waved his hand carelessly towards a chair, and took one himself when Victor was seated.

" I am prepared to hear the reason for your visit to me, Mr. Dufoy," he said.

" Oh ! sir," cried Victor, impetuously, " you know the reason that has brought me here. I have returned to claim Grace for my wife—to assert that my position is established—that the French Government has been lenient, and forgiven all old follies. I am prepared to take back Grace as my wife, hoping for that permission which you will be generous enough now to concede to me."

" It is not a matter with which I have a

right to interfere," said Abel, still more coldly. "I have done with the subject for ever."

"But Grace looks forward to your consent, sir; and believes that I have only to
prove my good faith, for you to grant that
favour which I ask."

"I give no consent to this match," said
Wrayford, sharply.

"I have a right, then, Mr. Wrayford, to
demand your objections to my marrying
your ward?"

"I have nothing to explain."

"And yet you," said Victor, "were my
benefactor—a kind, generous Christian, to
whose care and gentleness I owe my life."

"We need not prolong the discussion,"
said Wrayford, rising again—"I am tired of
it. I am busy, and have a task to fulfil before the sun rises."

"But your consent——"

"Does not stop the way to your marriage
with my ward," he said. "I am passive,
that is all. I will not utter one reproach at

a past deception ; but I do not pardon it, and I have no consent to give."

" What possible reason can urge you, Mr. Wrayford, to render your ward unhappy ?"

" Unhappy !" he repeated.

" What cruel stubbornness is it that steps between her happiness and mine, and makes you unworthy of yourself? Mr. Wrayford, is there a reason why you will not think of me or study her, or is this madness ?"

Abel Wrayford lost his presence of mind and all that cold demeanour which he had hoped would outlast the interview, and turned upon his handsome rival with eyes blazing with a long pent-up fury.

" Shall I tell you, Mr. Dufoy ?" he hissed. " Would you be glad to know the truth, all the truth, from which I have suffered ?"

" Yes, sir, I should be glad."

" You might regard this in another light, and go your way, if you were merciful," he said eagerly. "But, there—there, I cannot expect mercy or sympathy from you. Think me mad."

"No, I cannot withdraw now. Mr. Wrayford, I will respect your secret, but I ask you to trust me with it, for Grace's sake —in Grace's name?"

"And for Grace's sake you will keep silence?—you pledge your honour?"

"I pledge my honour."

There came a wild hope to Abel—a strange, wild hope—that Victor Dufoy would see that his love was very poor and weak in comparison with that which had been the one growth of his own life, and would retire before the greater passion.

"Then," he said, "I love Grace Edmonds!"

"You! you!" cried Victor; "yes, but as a father——"

"As a lover," interrupted he furiously— "as a girl whose progress from childhood I have watched, and for whose love I have waited, yearned for, prayed for."

" Great heaven !"

" It was her father's wish that she should not marry without my consent, she is aware, but she does not know—she will never know—that it was her father's wish that I should marry her."

" I see it all," said Victor to himself.

" I promised a dying friend that I would watch over Grace, that I would become her guardian, and teach her step by step to love me," Wrayford continued, with the same passionate excitement. " And with this thought before me, with my promise for ever ringing in my ears, with Grace growing up all that was beautiful and trustful, was it strange that I should link the one hope of my life to her, and let all other dreams go by? And when her heart was turning to me, and I had grown grey studying her happiness, when to lose her was like losing heaven, you came and took her from me.

Judge now, Dufoy," he said, with bitter emphasis, " how much I hate you !"

" Need this hate continue?" replied Victor, quickly. " Is it impossible to become my friend ?"

" We love one woman !" was the stern answer.

" But Grace——"

" Grace would have loved me had you not stepped between us—she would have turned to me again, guessing, at last, my long devotion, if you had kept away. And I deserved her more than you."

Victor made an effort to speak once more, and once more Wrayford interrupted him.

" You are a young man, with life before you, and there is a world of fair women to choose from. I have grown old in loving Grace, and she only is left me. Will you have pity on my isolation ?"

" I love Grace !" said Victor.

" What will you take to leave here for ever—to be heard of no more ?" said Wrayford, bitterly. "Will my wealth, my secrets, which will produce more wealth, tempt you to be merciful?"

"Sir, you insult me," replied Victor. "I love Grace. I would prefer resigning my life to acting dishonourably to her."

"I have no more to say," said Wrayford. "Quit my house before my resolution falters, and I hurl you and myself to perdition."

Victor looked up wonderingly at this remark.

"You are not safe here. Your life is a temptation to me—and I have grown very desperate. Go!"

"And your consent——"

"Is refused," cried Wrayford. "Will you leave my house at once?"

"I regret your obduracy," said Victor, sorrowfully; "but I have a hope that you will be just."

Victor bowed and withdrew, and Wrayford listened to his footsteps down the stairs and along the corridor, until the door closed

heavily behind him. Then he gave way
somewhat, and folding his arms upon the
table, he leaned his grey head upon them,
and sunk his grand scheme of distinction in
the depths of his sorrow.

CHAPTER IX.

ANOTHER SUCCESS!

ABEL WRAYFORD remained in that strange prostration for a longer period than he was aware; and it was only a startling innovation on his solitude that roused him from his reverie. He had thought all his life over again there, seeing where his fault had been, where his love had been too deeply hidden, and deceived his ward, and where her over-confidence and childish trust had allowed the rival to supplant him. So he had lost her, and even yet had not reconciled his mind to the loss. He was not generous enough to think of Grace before himself at present, although he believed that her felicity would have been with him rather than with Victor. The man's return had startled him, and his defence had shaken past convictions, but not utterly destroyed them. If he had only kept away —if Abel could have believed him a villain unto the end, and Grace have lived him down!

He thought of these things long into the night, forgetting his new scheme, so close upon completion, and the fame which was to follow its fair trial. This man of a great intellect, of whom the world was to talk one day, could think only of a girl's love, and see in her only his ambition. The wind and rain, and hoarse roar of the sea breaking on the beach below, spoke alone of Grace to his ears, and moaned with him at her loss; and the lamp upon the table lit up the student's grief, not his deep researches. The surprise of that memorable night was close upon him when he was brood-

ing still; but he had not met it yet. He
was unconscious that the door had opened
softly, and a man's head, rough, unkempt,
and remarkable for two great glaring eyes
within it, had peered round and vanished
again. He was not dreaming of intruders,
but of a fair-haired girl whom he had
pledged his word to a dying man that he
would marry; and when the wild-looking
head came round the door once more, his
own was bowed down, as it had been for
hours.

There were strange men in his laboratory
at last, rough-looking specimens of humanity, in heavy sea-coats and great boots,
who had entered with precaution, and were
now staring with a fierce kind of surprise
at the sleeping student. It was not till one
touched him on the shoulder that Abel
woke up to the new danger which was
threatening him, and sat back in his chair,
looking before him, and breathing very
hard.

Abel Wrayford was not a timid man, but the appearance in his room of these threatening figures was not to be received quite calmly even by a philosopher, or by a man who thought—or tried to think—that there was nothing worth living for in this world. The intrusion was so sudden and unlooked-for that Abel could almost imagine that it was a dream, a nightmare, from which he should start presently, and find himself alone. So deeply had this impression been made upon his mind that his first words were—

" Is this—real ?"

" It's real enuf," said a harsh voice, which he recognised, and which dispelled all fancy; "and you needn't be under no manner of alarm."

" Trustworth !" said Abel, quickly.

" Yes, it's me, guv'nor," answered Robert Trustworth, with an air of bravado that was a little forced—" it's me, the down-trodden,

druv to desperation by all the wrongs
you've put upon him."

" Why are you here?—what men are
these?"

"These men are my partikler friends—
old salts, who stick by me in my troubles,
and help me at a pinch; and the pinch has
come now, by all that's holy; and men must
live."

"I do not see the necessity," said Abel
Wrayford, contemptuously.

The chemist of Greymoor had recovered
himself, and had realized the danger in
which he was placed. There was a villainous plot against him; those men would
not have forced themselves into his house
and confronted him in this manner had
they not matured some cunning scheme by
which he was to suffer. They had taken
advantage of his lonely existence at last to
profit by it, and the desperate men at Greymoor, in whom he had not believed until
to-night, were about him in that house. It

was a question of robbery or of extortion; and he must hold his ground as well as he could against them, or, seeing the helplessness of his position, give in to their demands, if it were possible.

"We must live," said Trustworth, in a louder voice, "and one man must not have all the good things to hisself. You can't lord it over all of us like this, when there's lots of us don't know which way to turn for a bit of bread or a drop of drink. We won't have it no more without a fight for it —we're druv wild. Look at my friend Bill."

Wrayford looked in the direction which Trustworth had indicated, and saw in Bill a broad-faced, big-whiskered, scowling vagabond.

"There's a man, with nine children starving. He's druv to it with me."

"How much money do you want?" asked Wrayford. "Be moderate in your demands, gentlemen, for I have not much in the house."

"We know that. But you keep a banker," said Trustworth, with low cunning; "just as I did once, before the beggar bust up with 'arf my money—cuss him! And if you write us out a cheque, one of us will stop to cash it, whilst the others takes you out to sea until the money's paid."

"Out to sea?" muttered Abel Wrayford.

"And if there's a trick, and our pal gets into trouble," said Bill suddenly, in the hoarsest of voices, "we shan't stand nice about dropping you overboard; and, if all's square, why we'll land you in good time."

"No, that will not do."

"But it must do, Mister Wrayford," said Bill, who suddenly assumed the part of principal spokesman; "and you must come with us to-night. We ain't children; we ain't planned this for nothing; we ain't all like Bob Trustworth, chichen-'arted when the drink is out of him, and we've done rougher work than carrying off an old man like you for a sea-voyage."

"Who the devil are you calling an old man?" said Wrayford, testily.

In the midst of his danger he objected with all his force to the appellation. It was the title of "Old Wrayford' which had first suggested to Grace what a kind *father* he was to her!

"Mister Wrayford—if you like it better," said Bill; "and that's our mind, you see, to take you off. I don't see any safer way, myself."

"And the sooner the better," added the man who had not spoken yet.

Wrayford looked at the third speaker attentively, and recognised in him a man who had been imprisoned some years since for his share in wrecking a schooner with false lights. From these men there was no mercy to be gained; they had matured their plans, and he had been the object of much plotting, which, at last, had found its opportunity. The dark night was against him; the wind and rain were allies in these desperate men's favour—his own voluntary isolation had brought about his peril.

" I may as well be frank with you," said Wrayford, coolly. " I have not a heavy balance at my bankers, at present."

" I don't believe it," cried Trustworth.

" I have money in the Bank of England —money sunk in land, lent on mortgages— but not much money that can be drawn at sight. My balance is less than usual, owing to experiments which I have been carrying out."

" Wot's your balance ?" asked Trustworth. "Leave this to me, Bill—you've never knowed much about money matters."

" My balance is not more than a hundred pounds at present."

Trustworth swore violently at this statement, which he told Wrayford was a lie—a big lie, which would cost him dearly, for now Wrayford was trying to deceive him. Abel opened a drawer of the table at which he was sitting, and threw his pass-book towards Robert Trustworth.

"You have had experience in these mat-ters—judge for yourself."

Trustworth seized the book, and opened it eagerly. Abel Wrayford was right. The balance was one hundred pounds, fifteen shillings, and seven pence.

"Will that sum content you?"

Wrayford was prepared for that sacrifice —for a strange wish had come suddenly across him to be spared for Grace's sake, a strange fear also that he should be taken away by these villains, and be heard of no more, or that he might die in resisting the capture, and Grace, in mourning for him, would for ever think how hard and ungener-ous a man he had become.

"No, it won't do," said Trustworth, laying down the pass-book again. "Why, Wray-ford, you don't understand us yet. This is not a light business—a little business—a fancy of one or two of us. There's a boat in the cove, and there's a ship out yonder

waiting for it.   The ship breaks the blockade
at Charleston—you know about the war?—
and we're all going to offer our help as
sailors for the Confedder—Rats.   We go to-
night—and you with us.   But we want
money—two or three thousand—awful bad."

"I have not the money at my disposal.   If
I had, I should think twice of satisfying your
rapacity," said Wrayford.

"Well, you'll have plenty of time to think,
Abel Wrayford, for go with us you must.
We're too deep in this to start off empty-
handed, and we built on you."

"And if I refuse?"

"It don't signify.   We shall gag you and
carry you down to the beach," cried Bill;
"and if you disappoint us altogether, we
drop you over!"

"Let me consider this again," said Wrayford.

He could not see his way out of the trap,
and he could think only of Grace Edmonds
and her lover.   That he should disappear for

ever, and her remembrance of him for all
time should be only of his obduracy, of that
selfishness which had narrowed his heart
and wounded his ward's, was a thought
which rendered him as desperate as the
villains by whom he was surrounded. Why
could he not think of himself, of some plan
to secure his safety, or to bribe these men?
Why that pale, sweet face ever before him,
confusing those keen wits on which he had
prided himself before that night?

"Well?" said Trustworth, impatiently.

"Well," said Wrayford, compressing his
lips, "I decline to accompany you."

"By ——!" shouted Bill, advancing a step
or two towards him, as Wrayford rose in
self-defence, "how are you to help it?"

"I will not trust my life with you. I
would sooner, weak as I am, fight in my
own house for it," he said; "but I will make
you one more offer."

Bill paused, and Trustworth and his silent

friend in the wrecking line of business craned their heads forwards, all attention.

"I am anxious to remain in Greymoor, and I will not go to sea with you," said the chemist; "but I will show you that secret of the colour which has made my fortune, and can make yours, upon the condition of your departure afterwards."

"What's the good?" began Bill, when Trustworth touched his arm.

"Wait a bit. Let's hear him out. I know what that colour's brought him in, and what he would have been without it? Is it easy?"

"A child can understand it. And you, in America, can sell the secret for a large amount."

"We'll see if we can make it out fust," said Bill. "I don't believe in this game for a minit."

"You shall judge for yourselves—and you shall try the experiment for yourselves before you leave me."

"Blest if this ain't a rum start," said the third intruder, who had said little, but had intended a great deal; "are we going to stop all night? A hundred pounds is better than nothing; and I say take that, and his torpedo thing, which we can sell at Charleston; and him, too, till the cheque's cashed, and we get news that it's all right."

"Wait a bit," said Trustworth, "for——"

Then the three men conferred together in a low tone, inaudible to Wrayford, and quarrelled amongst themselves, he could see, as to what was to become of him, now that they had been disappointed in his banker's balance. He could see that they were not to be trusted for an instant, and that the danger would be no further removed from him after his revelation. Whilst they argued together, he thought deeply also; and Grace was in his thoughts again—Grace far away in that house across the valley, wherein the village of Greymoor nestled out of sight. In the house across the valley—the house from the windows of which he suddenly remembered his Nest could be perceived, and where Grace had spoken of her watch at times, in her concern for him; remembering also his promise that he would in a time of danger signal for help, if it were necessary! If he could make some sign, and if by chance Grace should draw aside her blind and look forth into the night, he might be saved to do her justice. He could but think again of what a hard-hearted, envious wretch he had become.

"Lookee here, Wrayford," said Trustworth, "we've talked it over. We will see the colour made, and if it's easy, we'll be square with you. There, that's fair."

"Very well," said Wrayford.

He opened a cupboard in his room, and took therefrom several bottles and phials, which he placed upon the table. Bill and his friend sat down on the floor, with their backs against the door of egress, and chewed tobacco solemnly; and Robert Trustworth looked at all the phials and their contents. It was a strange audience for a chemical experiment, and the half sullen, half vacuous look of the three seamen would have made Wrayford smile at a less momentous crisis of his life.

"I don't see how it is to be remembered," said Trustworth, gloomily ; "what's all that cussed gibberish on them bottles ?"

"I will explain presently."

"What are you up to with that light ?"

"I am making room for my experiment."

Wrayford had taken up his small oil-lamp, and placed over it a green glass, which he was accustomed to use at times, when his eyes were weak with over-application to his studies. This he placed, as if carelessly, on the sill of his window, and proceeded very quickly to direct the attention of his audience to the phials upon the table.

"A strong light affects my eyes, and disturbs my experiments," he said. "Now watch this piretic acid——"

" Piratic acid!" muttered Trustworth. " Bill, he's chaffing us. No games, Wrayford—you'd better not—upon my soul, you'd better not, old fellow !"

The experiment proceeded for awhile, Wrayford explaining, the men stolid, but attentive. Suddenly there was an interruption.

" I won't have the light there !" shouted Bill, with a vehemence that made Trustworth jump again ; " it looks queer to any one outside."

" It can't be seen from the village—it— why, dash it, though," cried Trustworth, " there's the coastguard lot, and the Lawsons, where Grace Edmonds is. By Gord, it's a signal—it's been arranged—we're done for if anybody's looking out !"

As Trustworth moved the light away, and the men at the door sprang to their feet, Wrayford stepped back to his cupboard, and to a small galvanic battery, which was

on the bottom shelf. An instant afterwards
he was at his table again, looking so deadly
white that even his enraged antagonists were
struck with his appearance.

" It is a trick, then," gasped forth Trustworth.

" I have not said so," answered Wrayford. " But you have doubted me, and the
experiment is at an end."

He swept the bottles to the floor with an
impatient hand, and regarded his persecutors with defiance.

"Tie him up, and take him away," cried
Bill; "we have not much time to lose;
and go he must—it's business."

" One moment," cried Wrayford in tones
which made them pause again, so clear and
startling were they. " Gentlemen, you are
losing valuable time, and every second
wasted here is a chance less for your life.
The torpedo is fired!"

Bill and his friend stared at Wrayford in

a bewildered manner, and Trustworth staggered back several paces as if he had been struck.

" Do you mean it, Wrayford—do you really mean it?" he asked, after two futile efforts to get his words out.

"I mean it," said Wrayford sternly. "Those wires in my cupboard communicate with a slow match leading to the torpedo buried in my kitchen. Time is allowed to quit the house, and only time, before the explosion. Doubt my word, stay here if you will, and the Lord have mercy on your wretched souls!"

He covered his face with his hands, and whispered a hasty prayer. When he looked up, the men were gone, and he could hear their heavy feet galloping madly down the stairs. One glance round, an instinct to gather up a few papers which were scattered on the table, and then he was following them with hasty strides. A minute afterwards and three men were running along the deserted cliffway, and the fourth, Abel Wrayford, making for the downward path leading to the village. He was already descending when he found that Trustworth and his associates had turned again and were gaining on him rapidly. He had no idea how weak he had become, and how incessant application to his studies had sapped his strength until he endeavoured to increase the distance between himself and his pursuers. Then he gave way, seized by an awful pain in the side that arrested further progress, and Trustworth's hands were on his shoulders.

"It wa—wa—was a trick, then," gasped Trustworth. "You can't go—we must take you away. It's more than our lives are worth to leave you in Greymoor."

"Coward!"

He turned and grappled with the fisherman, until the hands of the other were upon him and bore him to the earth. At the same instant there was a mighty roar, a trembling of the ground on which they stood, a bright stream of flame leaping up suddenly to heaven, and turning cliff, and sky, and sea to crimson, and then Wrayford's Nest was hurled into a thousand fragments.

They were thrown to the ground by the concussion, and Wrayford for an instant thought the sailors were dead, so still were they. Suddenly the scream of a woman brought them to life, and gave hope to Abel.

"He has destroyed the Nest," cried Grace. "Oh! haste, Victor—haste, good friends!"

There followed the tramping of many feet, and Trustworth and his men were on their legs again.

"The coastguard!" cried Bill; and with one bound he went to the cliff's verge and slid downwards like a huge cat, whilst Trustworth and his companion, holding their hands to their faces, disappeared in the darkness of the night that had followed the explosion, and were seen no more in Grey-moor.

Grace, Victor, and the coastguards, who had been aroused by Grace's energy, discovered only a grey-haired man lying on the wet grass in their path.

" Oh! Abel—my dear guardian!" cried Grace, bending over him.

" I am well—and safe," he whispered. " Let me rest a moment."

" You signalled to me? In the green light there was danger!"

" Yes. Thank heaven you saw it!" muttered Wrayford.

" What has happened?" asked Victor.

" I will tell you presently," he said, " the experiment has been tested, and—and the torpedo is a success."

" It has frightened Greymoor into fits, and broken all the windows in the place," grumbled Lieutenant Lawson.

" I thought it would," said Wrayford, drily. He was on his feet.

He made an effort to move after awhile, and when Grace and Victor drew his arms within their own for his support, he made no effort to withdraw them.

"I think that I have learned a lesson to-night," he said to Grace. "You were looking for me, then?"

"Yes. And seeing the signal, I found Victor, and——"

"Oh! he was not far off, I wager," Abel answered, in a cheery tone, that made their hearts leap.

"I found Victor, and we started off with those of the coastguard who were on duty."

"Saving my life," he said, "saving my life. Well, you came for me," he added, "presently, you must go to him."

"Oh! Gardy!"

"Oh! Mr. Wrayford!" exclaimed Victor, gratefully.

"Seeing you two happy—you two faithful lovers," he said, "I shall be happy myself, I think. Why, what will old Wrayford have to regret?"

He pressed Victor's arm, and Victor understood him.

Lower down the cliff they met all Greymoor coming up, with much whooping and shouting, towards the Nest. Abel did not appear to heed them, and when Grace said, laughingly, that here were more friends advancing to the rescue, he replied—

" My sight has failed me a little—I don't see them."

Grace and Victor looked eagerly into his face.

" Oh! he is blind!" she cried.

" Yes, yes; don't make a scene, Grace," he said, calmly. " Get me to Lawson's home, and there nurse me for a time. I may recover this shock in careful hands. That torpedo was very powerful. It is a great success, thank heaven!"

And in careful hands, and in the hands of her he loved, his sight came back slowly, after grave doubts of learned oculists. When he was well again, he gave Grace away at the altar of old Greymoor Church, which was not big enough for all those good neighbours who thronged the edifice to see the wedding. Robert Trustworth was not there. A man with only half a nose reached America about that time, in company with one gentleman who was thumbless, and another who was eyebrowless, and generally disfigured. They were sufferers by the war, they told folk who were curious—a little powder had blown up and damaged them.

Abel Wrayford nurses two of Grace's children now, and Victor, settled in England, helps him in his studies, as in those past days when he stole the chemist's hope away from him. And Abel as he bends his head over Grace's eldest girl—his hair is as white as snow now, and he is not forty-five—whispers again, as on that night they led him down the cliff, " What has old Wrayford to regret ?"

SENSATION AT SEASONVILLE.

SENSATION AT SEASONVILLE.

MERCENARY motives, sir! You may call them mercenary if you like, but I know better. I feel still that it was a respect for her reasoning faculties, and a reverence for her powers of debate, as exemplified in her Social Science paper of "Have Church-wardens Emotions?" as read before an enlightened audience at Mircham, that laid me a captive at her feet. Had she been the possessor of the mines of Golconda, without talent, sir,—real and indisputable talent—not a fibre of my heart would have thrilled to secure her. For it was not beauty that attracted me; she was *not* beautiful. It was

not form; she had no more grace of out-
line than a deal plank. It was not youth,
for although she was *not* fifty-one, as her
detractors were in the habit of affirming
—she came into her property at the age
of twenty-one, in the year of our Lord 1825,
for I have read her deeply-lamented father's
will very carefully over in Doctors' Commons
—still the bloom of the peach had been
lightly brushed aside by Time's relentless
hand. Young Griffin told me once that
" that did not matter very much, because she
had a lot more bloom in a box," which was
a coarse remark, and shocked me.

I am easily shocked, for I am of a sensitive and retiring disposition. And he intended to shock me ; but no matter. There
were reasons ; he did not like me ; he was
her second cousin, and she had expecta-
tions.

Let me repeat that it was a pure admir-
ation for her talents.

Had she been beautiful, graceful, and

youthful, I would have paused; for I was not—in all candour, I confess it—a Ganymede. Spiteful people called me an old bachelor, but they were a long way out in their reckoning. I had no love for isolation, and was sighing for a kindred soul who could share my heart, and home, and human sympathies, and who, with a little property of her own to add to my pension from the Custom House, would make my middle age and after life enjoyable.

I was not mercenary; I wanted talent; I was talented myself. I had written poems, and dedicated them to the crowned heads of Europe, and received answers the most flattering—poets are no worshippers of Mammon. Those poems, if they brought me fame, still cost me a deal of money, and I did not shrink from the expenditure.

Our ideas were in perfect accord; we were both sensitive, delicate minds, with acute perceptions of the Real and the True and the Sublime. We were thrown into each other's society a great deal at the *table d' hôte*, and at the drawing-room of the Royal Hotel, Seasonville, afterwards, and I felt that my time was come.

I was surrounded by enemies, and when it was discovered that Adelina had won me, I became the prey to such studied slights and indignities from Adelina's relations that my blood boils at their very recollection. Her nieces—some of them were grown up and married, and should have known better— surrounded her in shoals, and sought every opportunity to place me in a ridiculous light; they ran down my figure, and ran up my age, called attention to my false teeth—I would not have worn them if I could have helped —and tried to convince her that my hair was not my own, which I stood out for, as Adelina's mind was tender on the subject of baldness. She took my word for it, and never closely examined my parting.

I became the victim of many practical jokes—I call no attention to them. Great minds are above little indignities. Her relations even went as far as forgery in their revolting malice, and wrote as from Adelina, making an appointment on the pier at half-past nine, after the band had gone : and if the result was mortifying, I say little. Let it pass. Eugene Gratts can afford to forgive criminal malevolence.

From her male relatives, her brother in the army, her cousins, her nieces' husbands, I expected coarseness, and I got it. I was called an old fool by Major Batskin, and had duelling been in fashion, I should have stretched him a gory corpse on the sands at sunrise.

I was ironically complimented on my conquest by young Griffin, who was the only one ostensibly civil. I was looked down upon, cut on the pier, or laughed at by the rest of them.

But I loved Adelina, and I persevered. It was she who smiled upon me, who told me in confiding moments that she respected my motives, and regarded me as the most genuine of men. She was determined to remain in Seasonville, and she remained, and her relations took it in turns to keep guard upon her, and to decry me. They even went so far as to decry her at last, but they failed miserably.

"It's no use, Gratts, your dodging about here after my aunt; upon my soul, it is not," young Griffin said to me once in his usual coarse manner. "Lots of fellows have tried it on before—young fellows, too, and worth looking at—but she does not know her own mind for two months together; she's romantic, vain, and foolish, dear old girl, but she'll never marry you. She'll never marry anybody, I can assure you."

His assurance went for nothing with me —I despised it—he was all assurance. I told Adelina what he had said at the first opportunity—it was in Sims the pastry-cook's, behind a jelly-stand—and I urged her to fly with me.

She was angry with her cousin, but she would not fly; she had never wholly pledged her faith in me, she said—neither had she— but she had learned to value my sentiments, and every day was telling in my favour, and drawing us together by the tenderest and strongest of ties.

I again begged her to fly with me, away from my defamers and persecutors—I implored her to remember that she was her own mistress in every respect, and she wavered, and sobbed, and choked a little over her strawberry ice, and spoke of all her dear nieces and nephews and cousins, and of the impossibility of her lending herself to an act of deception as regarded them—as regarded, she added very prettily, herself.

For the third time I begged her to fly with me. We were the victims of a cruel plot, I said, and our enemies were legion. They spared no pains to make us ridiculous, and there was no necessity to study them. I grew very eloquent, Adelina Batskin had been never wooed in language so fervent and impassioned.

But she did not fly. I suggested that I should fly without her to town and get the license and return to claim her in the face of the world, and to march with her—her trembling hand upon my arm—to the altar steps—and she wavered and said that I might go at last.

It was a great success. In my mind's eye I saw the glory of my triumph, as I departed by the 6.45. Parliamentary next morning. The chiming of my wedding-bells was ringing in my ears all the way to London.

When I returned to Seasonville, two days afterwards, I discovered that the landlord of the Royal Hotel had let the bedroom which I had been accustomed to hire. It was an expensive room, and I had very naturally objected to pay for it during my absence in town. The landlord had not had the courtesy to reserve it for me, notwith-

standing my long stay at his hotel, or had
been bribed by Adelina's designing relatives
to play this contemptible trick upon me.
The hotel was full, and the landlord re-
gretted that he could not accommodate me.
It was race week—a fact which I had forgotten—and every room in his house was
taken. There had been excursions all day,
and he really thought that I should find
some difficulty in getting a room anywhere.
He should be very happy to take care of
my luggage until I was suited with an apart-
ment, and that was all that he could possibly do for me. I asked to see Miss Batskin,
but she had gone out with her brother to a
friend's ; he did not know where, and I said
very well, and went away, with my little
travelling-bag in my hand.

It was nine o'clock in the evening when I
set forth in search of apartments, undismayed
by the dismal prophecies of the landlord. I
was buoyant and hopeful ; the world lay
before me in its brightest colours, a path of

roses leading on to Adelina. I saw the
whole town from beginning to end, but I
saw no bills of apartments in the windows
of the houses, and that became a matter
for grave consideration after every hotel,
inn, and little beer-shop in the place had
declined to take me in. I awoke to the
consciousness that the town was not only
full, but absolutely overflowing; and as I
passed the railway-station again, and found
that the last train had arrived with a fresh
batch of people—three-fourths of them
sporting men, with their hats on one side—
the dreadful thought of what was to become
of me rushed with tenfold force to my
troubled brain.

I could not walk the streets all night. A
place must be found somewhere, at any
cost, before the town closed for the night.
They were already putting up the shutters
before the shop-windows, and every minute
was precious. I went along the parade once
more, without success; I tried every back-

street; I begged for mercy of the fishermen and boatmen in the "slums;" I fought with two men for the first possession of a knocker, from which was hanging a card with " A bed to let" written thereon, and I found that the card had been left there by mistake, the bed having been let to four gentlemen and a little boy three hours ago. I was weary, and forlorn, and despairing. Every house was full, the last train had gone, and there was no reaching the next town; people, with bags and trunks in their hands, were still plodding up and down the streets—what *was* to become of me?

I took advise of Mrs. Browser, at last; she came upon me like a flash of inspiration. She was standing at the door of her shop in High Street, cooling herself after the heat and bustle of the day. The shop was closed, but she had come to the door for a mouthful of fresh air, she said, the weather being warm and "muggy." I had never liked Mrs. Browser, for I had lodged at Browser's

last Summer, and been preyed upon, and
missed my tea and sugar, and felt that the
whole Browser family had lived upon my
ham; but she was a woman who knew
Seasonville. I asked after Mr. Browser;
he was poorly with the gout, and had gone
to bed; I hoped the little Browsers were
well; and they were very well, she thanked
me. I hoped that she could accommodate
me with a lodging till the morning, or that
she knew of some one who could accommodate me at any price, I added; for I knew
that Mrs. Browser was rapacious, and made
her harvest in these times, and I had grown
very desperate, and forgotten the value of
money. But Mrs. Browser only laughed
ironically.

"Lor' bless you, sir,"—she had a kind,
motherly way with her, which was very
deceptive until you knew her thoroughly—
"the whole place's been choked up since
five this afternoon. There's a greater sight
of people in Seasonville than I ever knowed

in all my life before.   Mr. Smithers has just
told me that they've actually let the bathing
machines, and that they're full of sporting
gents, who are swearing orful."

"Good gracious! what is to be done
now?"

"I should have been so glad to 'commo-
date you, Mr. Gratts," she said; "but it's
almost unpossible. There was a gent here
'arf an hour ago who prayed for me to make
him a bed in the shop, and to knock him
up at six, before we opened; but I didn't
know him, and I couldn't trust him with all
the goods about, not even for a soverin' and
a half."

The shop! It was a bright idea, and I
seized it with a comprehensive grasp. Why
not the shop? How much better than to
be wandering about the streets all night,
and looking in the morning, even in the
eyes of Adelina, as haggard as a horse. It
was a roomy shop—why not?

"But I am not a stranger to you, Mrs.

Browser," I said in my most persuasive accents; "and you would not be afraid of my running away with the goods. And for the sake of security, perhaps even a little less than a sovereign and a half——"

"Oh! I couldn't do it for less, sir, even if I thought of doing it at all," said Mrs. Browser, very sharply here; "for I should have to borrow some trestles and boards of Mr. Wilks, the undertaker next door, and pay him for them, and drag the bed from under my lawful husband, who's always ill the next day after sleeping on a mattress. It's only for the sake of old times that I'd undertake to do it."

"I'll agree, Mrs. Browser; I'll take the bed, with all its inconveniences; I'll pay the money. I'll be back in half an hour."

"Very well, sir; we shall be ready for you by that time."

I left my travelling-bag; I went away rejoicing. What were a sovereign and a half but thirty shillings' worth of triumph over crowds of my fellow-creatures despairing in the streets? I wrote a note to Adelina, begging her to meet me at seven on the cliff, and carried it to the hotel myself. The landlord was in the way; he promised to deliver my communication to Miss Batskin, and he hoped that I had been successful in obtaining a lodging, he said, with an ill-disguised expression of doubt upon his countenance.

"I have obtained a very comfortable lodging, thank you," I replied.

He did not believe it; he thought I was one of the bathing-machine division. I did not touch a scrap of food at his hotel; I went to an eating-house in the town, and fought my way to the counter with a mob of profane individuals, and snatched a hasty repast for one and threepence. Then I went back to Browser's.

My room was ready for me, and Mrs. Browser was waiting to bid me good night. I shuddered at the look of the shop. The

accommodation was poor, and the proper-
ties meagre and unstable.

Mr. Browser was a paperhanger and
general decorator. He was accustomed in
the day time to hang his last new patterns
from London over a rod in the window, but
the papers had all been rolled away, and the
shop was very bare and ghastly in its roomi-
ness. There was no counter, and I regret-
ted its absence, after a glance at the undertaker's trestles, which were depressing to
the spirits on account by their suggestiveness,
and alarming to the nerves of their appearance of fragility. On the trestles was a
shutter, a cupboard door, a piece of carpen-
try of some sort, and upon it was a bed and
mattress. For furniture I had two chairs,
one with a basin and ewer on it, and the
other supporting my chamber candlestick
and a glass of water.

"That's all I can do for you, Mr. Gratts
—it's humble, but 'ealthy—and it's only a
short harvest that we get in Seasonville at
race time."

" Yes,—it looks humble—and I hope it's healthy. It's a dreadful expedient, though, and I shall have some trouble to get into bed, I can see."

" It's as firm as a rock, sir."

" Very good."

" Any boots or things that you'll put out-side that parlour door shall be cleaned and brushed in time. We open at six, sir?"

" Yes—exactly," I said, with a nervous glance at the shutters; " and you'll call me at half-past five. I didn't remark a bar to those things. They are not likely to fall down in the night, I hope?"

" The boy that takes them down and puts them up is very careful. When they are all wedged in together, they fasten one another, like."

" Oh, do they?"

Mrs. Browser bade me good night, and wished me pleasant dreams. I thanked her, and in due course, after some acrobatic efforts, found myself on the top of my

trestles. I had put my boots and trousers
outside to be brushed for the morning,
double-locked the parlour door, placed the
chair against it for protection's sake, dropped
my teeth in the glass of water, as recom-
mended by the faculty, and hung my wig on
a nail that I had found in the window.
After all these precautions, I tried to sleep,
and failed, which was the more aggravating,
because I had a great deal to pay for it in
the morning. My mind was excited concerning Adelina, the shutter was exceedingly
hard on which I was stretched, and there
were the houseless and homeless visitors
walking up and down all night, and making
an unnecessary noise with the heels of their
boots. I dropped off to sleep at last, a long
sleep, chequered by strange dreams. The
trestles must have been on my mind as well
as beneath my body, for I dreamt that I had
been picked up in the street and carried to the
undertaker's to be taken care of till the in-

quest, and I felt that I was alive, but could not make Mr. Wilks understand that if he would kindly run into Mrs. Browser's, the whole matter might be satisfactorily explained. Then Adelina came to my rescue, and there was a struggle between Adelina and her brother the major, and young Griffin, with Adelina calling for the police, brandishing my marriage licence over her head, and telling them to respect the majesty of the law, at which they laughed so loudly that I awoke, and sat up in bed, with the laughter ringing in my ears still.

Heaven and earth, where was I? There were people shouting and shrieking with ribald laughter of the most terrible description, and it appeared as if I were in the middle of the street. I realized suddenly and completely the terrible nature of my position, and a cold perspiration began to bedew my brow. I had over-slept myself, or the boy of the shop had come before

his time and taken down the shutters. For
they *were* down ; I was lying in the full
light of day, like a Royal sturgeon waiting to be cut up by the fishmonger, and
twenty people watching me with their noses
flattened against the windows. I gave one
agonized shriek for Mrs. Browser, and dived
beneath the bed-clothes. How was I to
escape ? Who would put the shutters up
again and save me ?

"Shall I bring you any shaving-water,
sir ?" shrieked a boy.

"Ain't it time you were up, bald 'un ?"
roared another.

"Twig the governor's gums in the glass,"
said a third.

"Don't stand any of their chaff, sir ; fling
your wig at 'em," suggested a fourth.

"Hooray !" said number five, and a cheer
was set up which raised the street, and
brought another mob towards me.

What was to be done ? Where was Mrs.

Browser ? The crowd had rapidly accumulated; those who had been out all night were glad to exult over my painful position, and the shopmen from over the way and down the street were not slow to help them. I lay with the sheet drawn over my head listening to the comments of the people; their cruel remarks on my teeth—grinning themselves at my misfortune—their comments on my peruke hanging by a nail in the shop-window from which all the paper-hangings had been rolled, leaving a hideous profusion of daylight on the shop and me. If I could only reach the door and secure an indispensable part of my attire ; but Mrs. Browser, as if with fiendish malignancy, had placed my bed at a long distance from it, and I could not face the ordeal of walking in deshabille across the shop. I gave one more shout for Mrs. Browser, and the note was taken up by the unruly ruffians, now a hundred strong, on the other side of the

window-panes, and more hideous laughter
followed, and curdled every drop of my
blood.

A hand at last tapped on the door leading from the shop to the parlour, and Mrs.
Browser's voice—it was like the voice of an
angel to me—said in a high scream,

" Are you there, Mr. Gratts ?"

" Of course I am here, ma'am.   Oh, I am
so glad you have come !"

" Open the door, do.   Why didn't you
get up when I knocked ?" she asked, in tones
far from civil, and far less angelic.

" You   didn't   knock,   ma'am," I   said
severely.

" Do you know the boy has taken all the
shutters down, and that you might as well
be in the street, Mr. Gratts ?"

" I should think I did know it !" I shouted
back indignantly; and there was another
" Hooray !" from the crowd, and more fighting on the narrow pavement to get a good
view of me, and one boy was run over the

foot by a donkey-cart which was coming round with the milk.

"You're doing it on puppos, Mr. Gratts," screamed Mrs. Browser through the key-hole; "you're without sense or decency."

"Dammee, ma'am, tell your boy to put the shutters up!"

"He's gone for his holiday, and I can't find him anywheres."

"Tell somebody else, then."

"The boy has locked the shutter-box, and got the key, and won't be back till night. I shall have every window broke if you don't leave off making yourself a sight there, sir. It's shameful!"

"Tell the people to go away. Send for a policeman."

"Open the door and come out. There's all your things waiting in the parler."

"Mrs. Browser, I will not get out of this abominable bed in the sight of that wretched mob."

"I can't tell half what you are mumbling

about, Mr. Gratts, underneath them clothes!"
she shrieked.

I put my head out, and repeated my ulti-
matum ; and at the sight of my egg-like
baldness the crowd whooped, and yelled,
and danced, and one window cracked omin-
ously beneath the pressure.

" You'll have to pay for this, sir," cried
Mrs. Browser ; " I'll have the law of you."

" Where's your husband ?   Tell him to
hang something before the windows. Bring
a tarpaulin—put up his paper-hangings—do
something, woman !" I roared ; " I shall go
raving mad."

" My husband's in bed with the gout."

" Then do it yourself."

" I'm subject to swimmings—I can't go
up steps.   Come out, if you are a man."

" I will not come out.   This is an infa-
mous transaction—a plot of somebody's, and
you are all in it."

" Oh, you base insinuator !" screamed
Mrs. Browser, shaking the door, " you wick-

ed and depraved old man, to go on like this !"

She was a violent woman, and commenced battering the panels with her hands, but I would not get up. I knew how I should look to the raging mob, for I was very thin, and the little l had on was shortish. I should possibly, and speedily, go raving mad where I was, but there was no human power that could make me move while my reason was spared me.

" No," I muttered, rolling myself still more completely in my sheets, " let me die rather."

Mrs. Browser departed, and the mob continued to increase. The news of my terrible dilemma was circulating rapidly through the town, and I could hear people running from all quarters towards the house, just as if it were on fire. The hotels were turning out; the fishermen were coming from the beach; the market people were already there; the police of Seasonville were

nowhere in the face of a formidable mob,
and there was every probability, in another
five minutes, of calling out the military.

Suddenly there was a stir amongst the
people, some laughing and remonstrating,
and I, who was wondering if it were possible to enshroud myself in sheets and
blankets, and descend from my bed and
board and make for the door, peeped over
my counterpane and saw two flights of steps
and men upon them with a large tarpaulin
in their hands, borrowed from the corn-
chandler's. It was my own idea at last. I
saw young Griffin in the crowd, too, and I
heard him say, "Why, that's old Gratt's
wig, for twopence," as the tarpaulin was
held before the windows, and some cheerful
tapping with hammers commenced. I
breathed freer in the darkness, and I was
even stepping carefully out of bed, when
some barbarians made a rush at the bottom
of the tarpaulin, and dragged it from the
hands of those who would have spared my

delicacy, and whose heart had been touched by my distress.

I sprung back with a shriek, and covered myself hastily over, and, of course, there was more shouting and laughing in the streets. But the police were on the alert a second time, and once more the black covering was before the windows as a substitute for the shutters, which Mrs. Browser would not have tkaen out of the box.

That miserable woman's voice sounded through the key-hole of the parlour door again.

"Now, Mr. Gratts, will you get up or not?"

"Begone, woman!—I'm coming,"I shouted forth.

I leaped from my bed, seized my teeth, and dashed across the shop towards my wig. I was leaning over the shop-board, alle agerness and excitement, when—horror of horrors!—there was a cracking, and the tarpaulin of its own weight tore out the nails, and descended with a rush!

Oh! that last peal of laughter! I glared at my accusers; I heard a wild scream of amazement from a lady in a fly proceeding in the direction of the cliff to keep an appointment at seven; I caught a glimpse of Adelina fainting at the sight of me, I sprang wigless to the door, unlocked it, passed into the parlour, eliciting a scream from Mrs. Browser, who was retiring through the opposite doorway, and had not bargained for my celerity, slipped into my trousers and boots, and fainted with my head through Mr. Browser's portrait, which had been taken down last night to be cleaned.

When I recovered consciousness the crowd had departed, and all was over. All was over with me, too, for I was scarcely apparelled before a note, calm and dignified and heart-freezing, came to me from Adelina. It was as follows—

But no—I will not print it here. Her susceptibilities had been wounded, and her

trust had been misplaced.   She had believed
in my hair, and in my delicacy, and I had
deceived her.   "Farewell for ever!   Oh,
Eugene!" were her parting words.   I fare-
welled.   I was in Bayswater before dark.

JENNY MERTON.

JENNY MERTON.

FORTY years ago I was a supernumerary at the Royal George Theatre.
That honourable position in society was the
result of my "call" to the stage at the
early age of nineteen years. I had served
my apprenticeship to art on the floors of
barns, and in travelling Thespian conveyances
for many weary years. When Mogg's company broke up—old Mogg took to the fried
fish business in Whitechapel, and made his
fortune—there was another drop, and a
lower depth, and much groping about in the
shadows.

My father—a respectable grocer in the

country town of Fixature—was dead then, and the little money that he had left a rackety son had gone the way of all cash. I came to London as a last venture, and finally procured, after much hard fighting and frequent kickings into the street out of managers' sanctums, a supernumerary's berth at the Royal George Theatre.

I dragged on this kind of existence for three or four years, and then was discharged for getting drunk, and putting a " star " out in a crack speech. I tried the theatres due east after that, and picked up an engagement here and there at Christmas-time and Easter ; but it was slow, up-hill, heart-breaking work, and I had often to sleep about the markets, or under the dry arches of bridges, or in the warmest corners of deep doorways, when luck went dead against me.

Sometimes, in the very hard times, I have hung about the coach-offices—there were a few coaches still in the days of which I speak—and offered to fetch or carry anything; I have held gentlemen's horses; I have begged for halfpence; I have done everything but steal.

I went back to the George Theatre when the late manager became a bankrupt, and the theatre passed into fresh hands, and was engaged there, off and on, for years. I became one of the oldest supernumeraries, and had seen more great actors, and knew more anecdotes concerning them than any one in the establishment. They began to call me Old Whitedrop, and Father White-drop, and Everlasting Whitedrop when I was fifty-two years of age. I looked old enough, I daresay; if anything will make a man old, it is to live from hand to mouth, to have a week's engagement and a week's starvation, to exist behind the scenes day after day, and night after night, or, in some miserable Drury Lane garret, to write begging letters to lessees, and pray for mercy over them.

I was rather a favourite with my brothersupers, for I was a meek fellow enough, a capital subject for practical jokes, and did not mind running on errands, or copying music, or even doubling my part, when a comrade wanted to skulk, and the manager had gone home, and could not see what game we were up to.

I jogged on, always a ragged, miserable, half-fuddled fellow, fond of my half-quartern over the way, or a pinch of snuff from a liberal friend's box.

I took to snuff early in life. Every man has one absorbing passion—mine was snuff. It was a gigantic passion with me—I would rather have expended my last pennies in an ounce of rappee, than have had my roll and saveloy for dinner. I have often had to make the choice between them, and I have never given up the snuff. If by any chance I was entirely destitute, I used to beg for it of snuff-takers in the street, and a well-filled box has been the only thing my fingers have itched to snatch

at throughout the period of my long ad-
versity.

It was getting on to Christmas, and we
were working hard at rehearsals; there was
a great pantomime in preparation, and I
had twenty parts to play in it, and a busy
time of practice before me, and plenty of
bumps and contusions to look forward to,
my bones not being particularly supple,
and the clown being more than ordinarily
spiteful.

One morning I had taken a long pinch of
snuff at the stage-door, and was entering
the theatre very much refreshed by it,
when a little hand was laid upon my
arm, and a sweet voice said, close to my
side,

"If you please, sir, is this the stage-
door?"

I looked down, and there was a child
of ten or eleven years old, gazing up
at me—a poorly-clad, shivering little girl,
but with one of the prettiest faces I had

ever seen in my life. I was not much of an observer of strange faces or strange people; I had never been struck with the looks of any person before, that I could recollect, but there was something so *new* about this child, something so fresh, and innocent, and extraordinary, that when she repeated her question, I felt a tingling sensation all over me, and nearly dropped my snuff-box in my bewilderment.

"Yes, this is the stage-door," said I; "and what do *you* want here, young lady?"

"If you please, sir, I'm a fairy."

"Oh, you are—are you?" I replied, thinking how much more fitting she was to be a real fairy than a gaslight one; "you've taken to stage-life young, my child."

"Mother said there were many younger than I here."

"That's true, but, somehow, they don't look out of place like—like you will," I answered. "What's your name?"

"Jenny."

"Jenny what?"

"Jenny Merton."

" And you are really going to take to the stage ?"

" Yes, sir."

"Can you dance ?"

" Oh, yes!"

" You can ?—ah! it's no business of mine to interfere with any business of yours. This way—mind the step. God help you !"

I took her on the stage, where the rehearsal had already commenced, and left her to the questions of the ballet-master. I was soon deep in my small parts, and adding to my store of bumps and contusions by falling the wrong way and getting damaged. I tried not to bother myself about the child, but at times she would seriously disturb my peace of mind. I finished my day's allowance of snuff before the rehearsal was over, in my perplexity. When I was not "on," I leaned against the side wings, and watched her, thinking what a different being

she seemed from the pinch-faced, sunken-
eyed little waifs around her, and wondering
how long it would be before she grew up
like the rest of them.

It was a singular contradiction to the rule
that " people get used to everything," that
I never got used to Jenny Merton being
a stage-fairy.   It was more singular still
that a time-worn, stage-beaten old fellow
like me should take so great an interest in a
child of eleven years of age. On second consideration, I do not know whether it *was*
very singular, for she was always seeking
me out, and asking questions connected
with the " profession," and putting her
childish confidence in me about her home,
her sick father, and her hard-working
mother—in me too, an ugly little snuff-
taker, who had been passed over as
insignificant and foolish all his life !   Then
Jenny Merton used to remind me, with her
fresh, rosy face, of a little sister I had had
once— many, many years ago that was !—

who died when I was a boy, and who was
very fond of me to the last. Perhaps that
association drew me to the child more than
anything else did—but drawn to her I was.

She got on very well in the pantomime.
I daresay there were many said, " What a
pretty little girl!" from the front of the
house, as she skipped about the stage in
her gauzy dress and spangled wings. She
was engaged nearly the whole season.
There was generally room for a few children at The Royal George Theatre, and
the prettiest face had the best chance of re-
maining on the list when the pantomime
was over, and a legion of extras had been
dismissed. I left with the majority, but I
did not lose sight of Jenny Merton for the
few weeks that I was out of place. No, I
caught myself waiting late at night for her
at the stage-door.

One night a tall individual, in a seedy
great-coat, hung about the back entrance
of the theatre, and eyed me most sus-

piciously. There was a fair half-hour to wait before Jenny Merton would issue forth, and we spent it prowling round each other, and exchanging supercilious glances.

Jenny Merton arrived at last, and perceiving the stranger, ran towards him with a reproachful shake of the head.

" Oh! father, father, you should not have ventured out in this drizzling rain."

" It's too late for you to be out alone, Jenny. I never liked it, and now I'm well enough, I'll come and fetch you."

" But I never come home by myself, father," she said. " Mr. Whitedrop—ah! there he is—there he is!"

And her tiny feet came pattering along the wet pavement towards me.

" And who is this man, Jenny?" asked the suspicious father, advancing, and drawing his daughter from my side.

" One of the company, Mr. Merton," I hastened to reply. " An old man, sir, who, knowing the distance the child was from her

home, has often taken the liberty of looking after her."

"You're very kind," he answered; "but
why—my Jenny?"

"That's what I hardly know myself."

"Oh! he is such a dear kind man, father,"
cried Jenny. "He's been so very good to
me. It's old Mr. Whitedrop, the gentleman I have told you of before."

"Yes, yes, I've heard of him," said he,
still suspicious and distant. "And so you
are the man who sees my Jenny home? I
wanted to find out what——"

"What I was like?" I added, seeing that
he stopped abruptly. "Quite right, Mr.
Merton. I should have done the same myself."

We were walking on during this dialogue.

"It seemed strange, that's certain," he
muttered, more for his own benefit than
mine. "I can hardly make it out. It isn't
charity, it isn't for what is to be got out of
her. What is it for, I wonder?"

Jenny twitched him by the sleeve.

" Well, Mr. Whitedrop, what do *you* think of my Jenny's acting now ?" asked he, turning round with an abruptness that made me jump.

"She is a graceful little dancer."

"She'll get on,—eh ?"

"Get on ?" I repeated.

"She'll work her way through all difficulties—she'll become a star in time ! She has begun young, remember. She'll make her twenty, thirty pounds a-week some day ?"

" Bless my soul, Mr. Merton, you don't dream that she will ever get on at that rate, I hope."

He regarded me suspiciously again, and I lost the thread of my discourse.

" And why not ?" he asked, peremptorily. "The child is clever ; she has genius, plenty of it ! *You* know that well enough, or you wouldn't come dancing attendance upon her. We never do things without an ob-

ject in this world. Your hopes are far off
enough, but still——"

"Oh! father!" whispered Jenny.

"Far off!—ah! well, perhaps they are!
Dear, dear me, what was I saying?" I
muttered.

"You can't blind me about Jenny, Mr.
Whitedrop; it's no use attempting that," said
Merton, the rudeness of his behaviour increasing every instant. "You might deceive
the child, but not her father!"

"I don't want to deceive anybody."

"Bid Mr. Whitedrop good night, Jenny,"
said the man. "We're taking him out of his
way."

"Not at all," said I.

"Oh! yes, we are—you know we are!"
retorted the man. "*I* take care of her from
to-night, you understand! Bid him good
night, Jenny."

Jenny bade me good night in a low voice.
There were two tears in her large eyes as
she looked up at me. I returned her salu-

tation, and the surly father bore away his daughter.

I repaired to my garret in a bad temper —my feelings had been hurt, and my snuff-box was empty. I had been used to slights and insults all my life, and had in most cases received them with an equanimity of temper which was praiseworthy—but I felt this coldness somehow. I can't tell why I felt it so acutely at that time; it was very foolish of me.

I did not see Jenny for several months after that interview with her father; I did not think it necessary on my part to intrude upon Mr. Merton or the child, and when I got back to the "boards" I found that Jenny had been dismissed, her presence not being required either in tragedy or farce, which the Royal George Theatre had come out strongly in.

When she was re-engaged she came towards me on the first day of rehearsal, and, after shaking hands, said in her quiet voice, as if she were adverting to a topic which had been discussed within the last five minutes,

"You must not mind what my father says, Mr. Whitedrop; he's very fond of me, and a very good man when you thoroughly understand him. He was rude to you; but then he is—he is rather suspicious in his way. So's mother."

"There, don't say another word, Jenny," answered I; "it's not worth speaking about, my child. It was odd to be suspicious of me, though. But never mind." I took a hasty pinch of snuff to comfort myself.

"I know that I shall never be much of a star," cried Jenny. "I am so dull, too; but they will build upon my rising in the profession."

"Do you like the stage?"

"Not much—it makes my head ache."

"Do you like——but I won't bother you with questions, my dear. I'm a foolish old man, and too inquisitive for my age. There's

the procession going on. Where's my
banner ?"

After that evening, Jenny Merton and I
went our separate ways, and always bade
each other adieu at the stage-door. I found
Mr. Merton standing outside the door, night
after night, like a sentinel. He condescended to nod to me now and then, and,
as his suspicions wore away, or as he
found his daughter making but small
way in her art, or as he discovered by
degrees that the newspapers, which he
pored over in the tap-rooms of public-houses,
totally ignored her existence, he became
more friendly in his manner to me ; we even
got to shaking hands a little before Boxing-
day ; but when I ventured to offer him my
snuff-box, in a moment of rash confidence,
he drew back with his old suspicious look,
and was reserved for the remainder of the
week.

Two years passed away thus, Jenny
growing prettier and prettier, and I be-

coming more stage-beaten, and more of a shrivelled, snuffy-looking old man. Jenny was no more popular than on the day of her *début*, a natural consequence enough, although Mr. and Mrs. Merton could not readily account for it. The two years were getting on to three when Jenny Merton was taken ill. My affection for the child had known no diminution—nay, had become the more powerful for the studied coolness of her castle-building father; therefore a natural desire to learn how she was progressing, and whether the fever by which she had been attacked was increasing or diminishing, led me to brave the freezing reception of her parents, and to call at the home of the Mertons in Little Choke Street, Drury Lane.

Jenny was no better. I called the next day—she was worse; I called three times on the day following, and my real solicitude for her, my more than natural yearning to see her, to try to cheer the weary moments

Q 2

spent on her sick-bed, made some impression on her parents, and I was admitted within the precincts of her home.

The father, the mother, and I had many long conversations together about Jenny, whilst the girl lay sleeping in the little room upstairs. Mrs. Merton was as suspicious of evil influences keeping back her child, and as sanguine of that child taking the world by storm some day, as her silly husband. Why should there be a doubt of the child's getting on—so pretty, so graceful a dancer, so clever as she was?

For some time I was puzzled to discover a legitimate reason for these sanguine aspirations, but it oozed out one day. It appeared that there was a Merton in the family who had taken to the stage some forty years ago, who had risen to the top of the tree, and had died, bequeathing a large fortune— much to the disgust of his relations—to a missionary society!

It had come into the heads of this foolish

couple—fostered by the idle words of a supernumerary like myself, lodging in the cellar—that their daughter Jenny had inherited her relation's histrionic talent, and that another Merton was destined to a successful career upon the stage. They had determined to begin early, and so they had commenced with a dancing-master in the next street. Jenny was quick enough at her lessons, and her parents snatched at this as at a promise of future excellence. Visions of benefit nights, crowded houses, heavy rains of bouquets, a carriage and four, a deputation of managers, testimonials of silver teapots and diamond bracelets, MISS JANE MERTON in the biggest of capitals on every dead wall, floated before the eyes of the visionaries, and sustained them in their poverty. The Mertons were print-colourers for a publisher of children's books, and made money in their busiest times; but the greater portion of the proceeds were set apart for Jenny's dancing-master, and Jenny's white muslin dresses, satin boots, and kid gloves. Patience—she would pay them a thousandfold some day—all in good time, all in good time.

Jenny Merton's fever nearly put an end to these ambitious dreams by carrying away the object of them, but her youthful constitution finally overcame the disease, and she grew stronger. As she increased in health, the old reserve and suspicion of the parents increased likewise; so that, finding my welcome at Little Choke Street only visible in the child's eyes, I gave up my customary calls and went back to my solitary home. The Mertons did not want any hangers-on to the skirts of their daughter when she rose to the pinnacle of fame. They saw the game that I was playing; they did not blame me—it was natural enough—but they were people of the world, and not to be hoodwinked in that manner, at their time of life.

I left this couple of monomaniacs to form

their own opinion of me without any opposition by sound argument. It did not matter
to me so that I saw Jenny at the theatre,
and she did not throw me off, and her head
was not turned by the family chimera. Jenny
was a sensible girl, and estimated her
parents' hopes at about their just value;
but it pleased the Mertons to see her on the
stage. She made a few shillings at Christmas,
Easter, and Whitsuntide, and was only in the
way at home. She was an innocent, light-
hearted, gentle girl, but not a genius.
She grew up very fast; the years drifted
rapidly by; before I could believe it she
was a young woman, too big and too
pretty for the establishment of the Royal
George Theatre. I did some good as a
counsellor in her choice of friends. I
pointed out the black sheep in our flock—
there were a few of them. I watched over
her very closely—even jealously. I was as
careful about her companions as though
she had been that little sister of mine who

had died when I was by many years a younger
man.

Jenny grew up a reserved and modest
girl—she grew up very beautiful. At seventeen she was permanently engaged at the
theatre ; she was handy as a waiting-maid,
a page, &c. ; and was always the fairy-queen
at Christmas. She had little speeches to
recite occasionally, and she got through
them so well that her parents fully believed
in her star rising at last. She only required
some disinterested friend high in the profession to push her forward, in order to prove
to the manager that there was great genius
in her, biding its time to take the British
public by storm.

It was a custom at the George Theatre—
and a custom not very uncommon at any
theatre in those bad old days—to allow friends
of the manager, or patrons of the establishment, to lounge behind the scenes, and idle
away their time at the side-wings, hand and
glove with the great actors, and familiar and

facetious with the prettiest of the supernumeraries.

Jenny Merton, by her discretion, kept the
majority of these would-be admirers at a
distance; but there was one person who
afforded her considerable anxiety, and caused
me and others no small amount of excitement. This was the honourable and younger
son of Lord Boddles, a dashing, free-and-
easy, dissipated young scamp of one-and-
twenty. He was a source of alarm to everybody on the staff of the Royal George
Theatre. He was not quiet for a single
moment. There were two supernumeraries
in the secret pay of the manager engaged to
keep a constant eye upon him, and they
could not. He was as full of practical jokes
as a monkey. One night he sent me before the
public with a dirty cloth pinned to the end of
a brigand's green velvet jacket, and exposed
me to roars of laughter from the whole
house; he was constantly sparring up to
Sparks, the first comedian, and hitting him

on the nose; he would send round on Saturday night a dozen of wine for the ladies of the ballet, and come in with reeling steps to draw the corks; he was partial to waltzing with anybody whom he could seize round the waist; and he had a very strong *penchant* for pretty Jenny Merton. He was a nuisance to the whole establishment, but he was a patron, and to be relied upon for ten pounds worth of benefit tickets at any moment. Poor Jenny was naturally alarmed at the attentions of the Honourable George Boddles—she hid from him in her room, or kept close to the prompter when her duties compelled her to the side-wings; and more than once I have been the shield between her and the Honourable, and have had to put up with a remarkable amount of abuse for my officiousness.

It was only natural to suppose that the Honourable George Boddles was as much an object of solicitude to his friends and relations as to the manager and his staff, therefore we were not surprised to find his father, Lord Boddles, occasionally at the back of the stage, making inquiries for "George," and using every means in his power to induce George to go home.

Lord Boddles was a stout little man, with grey hair and gold spectacles—a waddling, pompous little fellow, who always wore a long sky-blue coat, with gilt buttons, and a pair of tight-fitting black pantaloons. Lord Boddles had not borne the most reputable character in his young days —indeed, he was not entirely free from public aspersion at the time of which I write; but, then, everybody knows what public aspersion is.

It was Lord Boddles who condescended to accost me one Saturday evening.

"Man."

"Did you call, my lord?"

"Where's Stonger?"

Stonger was the lessee, by the way.

"Not here to-night, my lord."

"Then go and tell Racket I want him."

Racket was stage-manager, and a very good manager too.

"Mr. Racket has gone home, my lord."

"Dear me! dear me!" said he, in a fidgety manner. "Here, you sir, don't go. You'll do as well as anybody else. Where's the Honourable George Boddles?"

"Talking to the fairies, sir."

"Tut tut, tut!" exclaimed his lordship. "Shameful, shocking, shameful! Have you been long at this house?"

"Off and on, some fifteen years, or thereabouts."

"There's a sovereign for you."

You might have knocked me down with a feather. A sovereign!

"Now don't mention to a soul what I am going to say—do you understand?"

"Perfectly, my lord."

A sovereign! What a heap of snuff it would buy!

"My misguided son, the Honourable

George Boddles, spends half his life hanging
about this sink of iniquity, does he not?"

" He's very often in the sink, my lord."

We could see the stage from our position
at the wing, and at this moment Jenny
Merton went dancing to the footlights, with
half a hundred of the *corps de ballet.* Lord
Boddles, pointing at Jenny with his gold-
headed stick, asked—

" Who's that girl?"

"That's Miss Merton, my lord."

" Now, in my solicitude for George—that
is, the Honourable George Boddles—it has
struck me that that girl is an especial mark
for my—for the Honourable George Boddles'
notice."

" Ah! it has struck me too, my lord."

" Oh! has it?"

" It would be a sad thing for the family
if my—if the Honourable George Boddles
were to run away with that pink-faced
hussy," said he; "and if she were to in-
veigle him into a——"

"No fear of that," I said, very sharply. "She's a good girl, the best of girls, my lord, and is only too anxious to keep out of his way."

"Ah ! that's cunning."

"No, it isn't."

"Well, well, well," he replied, hastily, "you have your ideas of human nature, and it is not for me to argue the point. Now I want you, despite your belief in the purity and innocence of—what's her name?"

"Jenny Merton, my lord."

"Of Jenny Merton," he continued, "to keep a strict eye on the actions of her and the Honourable George Boddles, and to inform me, by letter or messenger, of their goings on."

"Goings on !" I muttered, indignantly.

"Of course I shall reward you for your information," said his lordship.

"Very well, my lord, I'll look after him."

"And what's your name?"

"Whitedrop."

" That will do—I shall remember it."

He took his departure, leaving me some-what puzzled with him. Why he should place especial confidence in me was more than re-markable, unless he had observed at any time that I was a friend of Jenny's, or that Jenny Merton had always something to tell me between the parts about her father, mother, or home. As for his interest in his son, although it was natural enough, still I thought that I discovered an extra rea-son for it in a newspaper paragraph which I came across soon afterwards, and which spoke of a probable match between the Honourable George Boddles and Lady Mar-garet Millicent Millionacres, of Millionacres Castle, Shropshire, a lady who had been thrice a widow, and was then in blissful pos-session of the four largest estates in the kingdom.

I kept close watch on the Honourable George Boddles after that evening. I was often distressed at his boisterous behaviour, and his perseverance in following poor Jenny; but I could not detect any "goings-on" worthy of informing his aristocratic parent.

I had another subject on my mind which was infinitely more distressing to me. This was in the shape of young Ned Heartworth, a fiddler in the orchestra. He called himself a violinist—I never owned him to be anything but a fiddler. He was a general favourite in the house; I could not tolerate him at the time, and it was a long while before I took a liking to him. I had my suspicions of him from the first. I very quickly detected his eyes wandering towards Jenny Merton, and knew how often he lost his place in the music-sheet, and fiddled away extemporaneously. He sometimes attended the rehearsals, and on those occasions he behaved in the most designing manner, coming on the stage and addressing Jenny—he used to stammer and blush, when he talked to her, like a great girl—

asking unnecessary questions about the parts, the time of the dances, etc., solely to hear her musical voice in reply. The young ladies and the few black sheep teased Jenny about Ned Heartworth, and she coloured and was indignant at their jests, which were bad signs; and Ned Heartworth began to bring flowers from his own garden—Hackney-way, he said—and Jenny used to take them home with her and keep them in a vase in the little top window of her room, which was a worse sign still. I soon discovered that Ned Heartworth did not live Hackney-way at all, but bought his flowers at Covent Garden Market, which completed the villainy of human nature, and set me taking snuff by wholesale.

Jenny never mentioned Heartworth to me—another bad sign this—and if it had not been for my own observation, I should have been unconscious of the fellow's existence. Heartworth bore a very good name for his abilities, and was a favourite with his brother-musicians; but the more I heard in his praise the more I disliked him. I watched him more closely than ever I did the Honourable George Boddles. When it came to Heartworth dangling behind the scenes between the parts, waiting for a word from Jenny—when it came to my meeting him and Jenny one Sunday afternoon in St. James's Park, and to seeing them feed the ducks with biscuit, I thought I should have broken my foolish old heart. I thought, also, it was quite time to put a stop to it, and so early on the Monday evening I waited for Jenny Merton's coming to the theatre.

" Jenny," said I, " I want to ask you a few questions."

" No one more welcome to ask them than you, Mr. Whitedrop," answered Jenny.

" No one?"

She blushed, but repeated the assertion, adding the hope that I did not doubt her word.

" Jenny Merton," continued I, " what I

am about to ask, you have no right to answer—you have even a right to tell me to go about my business, and to mind it instead of yours. But I don't think you'll do that. I knew you when you were such a little girl, Jenny—you are the only one I have ever thought or cared for since I became an actor, and my sister died. Now, for the sake of our old friendship, Jenny, will you tell me?"

" Yes, I will."

" That's spoken from your true young heart," I said. " Can you guess what I am going to ask you, Jenny?"

" I think I can."

" I am going to ask if you think anything of Ned Heartworth?"

Her face flushed, but she replied in a steady voice,

" He is very kind to me—he likes me very much. I cannot help thinking of him, Mr. Whitedrop, or of liking him in return.

R 2

He is a very good young man—he is very
fond of me."

I kept taking snuff so rapidly that it
frightened her.

"Ah! me, I'm sorry to hear it, Jenny—
there, it's all gone."

"What is?"

"Nothing—snuff."

"I have been going to tell you once or
twice, Mr. Whitedrop, for you—you are
so old a friend, but I could not find the
courage."

"Does your father or mother know of
this engagement?"

"I have not mentioned it yet," answered
Jenny. "Ed—Mr. Heartworth is going to
speak to father himself; who I don't think
will listen to him—heigho!"

"Why not?"

"Father builds upon my distinguishing
myself in the profession!"

"Do you fancy that he would refuse his

consent to your engagement with Mr. Heartworth?" I asked.

"Oh! yes, I am sure of it," answered
Jenny; "although Mr. Heartworth is so
much above me. Why, his mother has
a shop in King Street, and yet he is not
proud."

" Mr. Heartworth must ask your father's
consent, Jenny, at once. Perhaps he'll
bring him to reason—if there's any reason
in him. I can't give advice—*I* can't tell
you what to do—I am a miserable, ugly
old wretch, without an idea. I'm a rascally
old fool!"

And with these vehement exclamations, I
ran into a tobacconist's, and spent my last
penny.

A week after this dialogue with Jenny
Merton I observed that she was very thoughtful and low-spirited, and when I went
before the audience as one of a grand
assemblage of villagers, I instinctively glanced

at Ned Heartworth for the reason. There
he was, in the orchestra, as white as a sheet,
fiddling away in an absent manner, and
frowning at the music-page as if it were a
death-warrant. Jenny came on during the
scene as an attendant to Miss Cruncher, the
great actress, and Heartworth brightened
up a little whilst she was on the stage.
They exchanged one quick glance of affection, I thought; but it might have been
fancy. I had been full of fancies lately.

I found no opportunity to question Jenny
that night; it was a busy time of marching
off and on, and in my spare moments at the
side of Jenny, the Honourable George Boddles kept hovering so near, and keeping up
such an incessant state of stare, that there
was no getting a word of quiet conversation
from her.

The next morning there was too much
fagging at the rehearsal of a new piece to
afford time for any confidence on Jenny's
part. Richard Warnham, the great trage-

dian, was engaged for fifty nights, and this
was the first day of his rehearsal. What a
wonderful man he was! How beautifully
he could feign rage and despair, and devouring jealousy and all the passions of
humanity; what salaries he took; and what
grand airs he always gave himself! He was
a very great man; he drove up in his carriage and pair to the stage door; he turned
up his nose at the actors on the establishment, and gave one finger to the lessee to
shake. What impressed *me* more than anything was his diamond snuff-box—such a
snuff-box—it held three quarters of a pound
at least!

Warnham was a fine man, but a trifle
baggy in the cheeks. He was quite an aris-
tocrat in private life. He did not bear a
very excellent character; it was whispered
that he had broken the heart of his first
wife. and had so ill-used his second that
she had run away with Captain Fitzlight, of
the 107th, in sheer self-defence. Warnham's

engagement was not many days old when
his rolling black eyes were turned in Jenny
Merton's direction.   Warnham deigned
even to address Jenny, and was astonished
to find the object of his attention more
frightened than flattered.   I guessed pretty
well what kind of annoyance Jenny Merton
would have to put up with during his fifty
nights' engagement.   There was no denying
it, Jenny was not fit for the stage—no pure-
minded, modest girl was, in those days, for
the matter of that.   Pestered by Warnham
and the Honourable George Boddles, and
harassed by her own unprosperous love affair,
the poor girl's life became a misery.

It would be hard to part with Jenny.   I
had not been the same man since our
first meeting at the stage door; but she
was better away from the theatre; there
was danger lurking in her path, and I felt
that I must try to save her from it.   Actu-
ated by a sense of rigid duty, I called one
afternoon at her father's house in Little

Choke Street. Jenny was not at home, which was all the better for my project. Merton and his wife were in the front parlour, colouring prints and themselves very diligently. I broke the ice at once; there was no use beating about the bush with people of their calibre.

" Well, Mr. Merton, I suppose you have given up all idea of Jenny's turning out a genius by this time ?"

It was rather a rough commencement, but I thought it was better not to study refinement with these Mertons.

" Have you come all this way to ask me that?" he said bluntly.

" Not exactly."

" Then what have you come for ?"

" Your Jenny has had a long apprenticeship to the stage," I began, " and as an old actor, I may venture to say that she will never rise higher than she has done. She makes a neat waiting-woman, and a good fairy-queen—that's all."

"That's all you know about it," grumbled Merton.

"As true as I am standing here, it's the plain truth," I said, earnestly. "She is too good for the stage; she's too pretty—more than that, she is exposed to too much—I will not say temptation, for she is above it—but to too much danger. You are her parents—why don't you look to this more?"

Mrs. Merton turned pale, but her husband gave an angry grunt of disapprobation.

"Ah! it don't do, Mr. Whitedrop," said Merton, "it don't do, I tell you. I can't exactly see the drift of your argument, or understand what the deuce your game is; but I have always had my doubts of you, and shall have to my dying day. You're a deep one!"

I bore up against this vile abuse, and took refuge in my snuff-box.

"Why, we went to the play ourselves only last week and saw her, and she is getting on wonderfully," continued Merton. "She only wants a friend to help her on now. I shall drop a line to Warnham."

" No, don't do that!"

" What, you are afraid of getting expelled for your underhand proceedings, are you?" he exclaimed. "There, Mr. Whitedrop, we've done with you for ever. Good day, you've got over Jenny somehow with your artfulness, but you're no true friend to us or her."

" It's no use talking," I exclaimed despairingly, " you are blind to good advice, and you can't think for yourselves. You'll have to rue it, though—you'll have to rue it presently!"

I thrust the snuff-box to the depths of my pocket, and ran out of the house.

I did not think that they would have to rue it quite so soon, or that the day had already dawned for much mystery and trouble. I remember that night was Warnham's benefit night, and there were extra pieces, and plenty of hard acting in them. Jenny did not perform in the last farce, and took her departure half an hour earlier than myself. I remember also that it was very late when I got home, and one of the windiest nights that I had ever known. I found no rest in my garret, with the window clattering furiously in its frame, and the wind shrieking, whooping, and yelling over the house-tops, and keeping me from sleep, despite the long fagging night that I had had of it at the theatre. I sat up in bed and finished my snuff as a last resource against these horrors —then I thought of Jenny Merton—then a chimney-pot was blown off the roof of the next house but two, and smashed into a thousand pieces on the pavement, and finally there came a sudden noisy knocking and banging at the street-door below.

"I wonder who that is?" thought I, "somebody from the country for the man in the parlour, or the second-floor-back come home drunk, or some one knocked down by the chimney-pot, and they want to bring him in here—dear me, what an awful noise they are making!"

They kept at it too; so, despite its being no business of mine, I got out of bed, forced open the window, and thrust my head out to expostulate against the uproar. The wind immediately whisked off my nightcap, and nearly blew me backwards into the room. Whilst I was holding on to the window-sill, and seeking to recover my balance, I heard a voice from the story below say,

" What the deuce is the matter?"

" Does a man—Whitedrop—live here?" were words heard mumbling with the wind.

" Who?"

"Whitedrop—an actor—George Theatre?"

" I can't hear a word you say—damn the wind!"

And the speaker banged down the window, and put an end to further conversation.

I had caught at the name more quickly

than my fellow-lodger, and having obtained a good hold of the sill, I ventured to lean out.

" What is it? My name's Whitedrop. What is it?" I called below.

" Is anyone up there ?"

" Yes. Whitedrop," I yelled.

" Is your—name—Whitedrop ?"

" Yes."

" Please—down—then."

" I'll come directly."

I don't know whether they heard me, but they left off knocking. I shut the window, slipped into my clothes, and put my empty snuff-box into the tails of my coat-pocket. After I had groped my way down stairs in the dark, I proceeded to open the door. Three men instantly tumbled in, and two of them roughly collared me.

" What's the matter?"

" You must come with us—we're police officers—it's no use struggling."

" What have I done? I'm not going to

struggle. Who charges me with anything?"

" I do, you artful, scheming, villainous old rascal !" shouted a voice I knew. " I do, you snake in the grass !—you wretched, black-hearted viper ! Give me up my child ! You know where she is ! You're in the plot ! You have something to do with it ! Where's my daughter ?"

"Oh ! Mr. Merton, I hope no harm has come to Jenny."

" Take the hypocrite away."

" But Jenny ?" I cried. " Do tell me what you mean, and I'll go peaceably any-where. Has—hasn't she come home ?"

" You know she hasn't."

" Oh ! dear, dear me !—O Lord !—oh ! Jenny, poor Jenny ! Oh ! what is to be done ?"

There seemed nothing to be done in my case but to suffer myself to be walked to the station-house, to be charged with the abduction of Jenny Merton—her father seemed to swear to anything in his rage—

and to be finally thrust into a dirty police-
cell, already tenanted by a drunken Irishman and two young thieves. What a
host of torturing thoughts kept my mind
on the stretch all those weary hours of
inactivity. Jenny not at home—stolen
away, eloped, perhaps, with young Heartworth! No, no, she would not do that. I
knew her too well. Oh! where was she?
Oh! Jenny, Jenny!

I rapped my skull against the wall. I
held my head between my hands, and
shivered with the worst of fears. I prayed
for her as for some one very dear to me.
And, ah! no one but God and myself know
how dear she was to me; dearer than that
sister who died when she was young; dearer
than my own purposeless existence; dearer
than all the world in my eyes!

And she was missing, perhaps dead, perhaps in the power of some unscrupulous
villain. Let me out!—let me out!

The Irishman and the two young thieves

know how I spent the next four hours; I have no perfect recollection—nothing but a dreamy idea of choking myself with sobs, of kicking against the door, of knocking my head against the wall, and of opening an empty snuff-box.

I was carried away, at last, into the streets, and round to the Police Court, and into a little wainscot pew, from which I could see the magistrate at a table on my right, half-a-dozen policemen hanging about the opposite doors, a reporter beneath me, sucking the end of a lead pencil, Mr. Merton facing me in the witness-box, and a few stragglers in the body of the court, amongst them young Heartworth, very pale and nervous.

Mr. Merton began his statement, but his agitation and rage would not allow of a clear statement of the case, despite the magistrate's injunctions to keep cool and take his time. After a deal of blowing and snorting, and wiping his forehead with his coat-sleeve,

he got through his case, which accused me
of being in a plot against his daughter, and
of carrying her away. He related her mysterious disappearance, and entered into a
minute account of my visit to him yesterday
afternoon, dwelling upon the dark threat
with which I had left him.

"What have you to say?" said the magistrate, looking at me.

"Speak out," said a clerk at my elbow.

"I have nothing to do with it," I cried.
"I am more concerned than anybody here.
It was my interest for her safety that made
me beg of him to take his child away from
the theatre and the persecution of bad men.
I have dreaded something like this—I have
warned him of it."

I said a great deal more in my defence,
and begged to be set free, that I might try
my best to find her.

Heartworth here forced his way to the
witness-box, and pleaded somewhat inco-
herently in my defence. He knew Jenny

Merton well—she had always spoken in the highest terms of my affection for her. I was a poor, inoffensive old man, generally believed to be a little out of my mind, but as harmless as a baby.

There was no occasion for that general belief; but I looked over it, considering the present state of his own mind, poor fellow!

This was the first day I had ever arrived at a just opinion of Ned Heartworth. He was not such a bad young man, after all; although he had no right to fall in love with Jenny Merton.

The magistrate asked a few questions of Heartworth as to his knowledge of Miss Merton, and then said,

"It is a mysterious case, and must be rigorously inquired into; but I see no reason to detain the prisoner. He was found at home in his own house, and was evidently astonished at the accusation brought against him. He appears to be a man well known for his simplicity and good feeling. An

officer has just returned from the George
Theatre, and has learned that the prisoner
did not leave the theatre for upwards of
half an hour after Miss Merton had taken
her departure. The prisoner is discharged."

I was led out of the witness-box; but not
into the street. I found myself ushered
into a neatly-furnished room, where the
magistrate and two or three sharp-looking
gentlemen awaited me. They made some
minute inquiries as to the names of the individuals in the habit of frequenting the
theatre, and took special notes of the names
and addresses of Mr. Warnham and the Honourable George Boddles. After a few more
questions, varied by considerable muttering
between the sharp-looking gentlemen and
the magistrate, I was at liberty to go home,
and go mad if I liked.

I found Heartworth lingering in the
streets. Upon seeing me, he caught hold of
my arm, and hurried me along.

" Where are you going, Mr. Heartworth ?"

" I don't know—I don't care—anywhere."

" Is there—is there any occasion to walk so fast ?"

He relaxed his speed, and began to groan.

" We mustn't give way yet, Mr. Heartworth."

" *We !*" he cried—" what have *we* to do with it? What share have you in my agony, or in my awful suspense ? You cannot imagine half the horror in my thoughts, half the racking at my brain !"

" Yes—yes, I can. Don't speak any more about that, if you please !"

" If *he*—her father—had not refused me his consent, but had let me take her away from the cursed stage, this would not have happened. Oh ! we should have been so happy ! I loved her so, Whitedrop !—I loved her so very, very dearly !—I—where are you going ?"

" Snuff !" I cried, in a choking voice, and ran across the way.

My feelings were composed by the time I

returned to Heartworth, who was pacing up and down, like a wild beast, before the tobacconist's. I offered him my replenished box, but he pushed it abruptly away, nearly knocking snuff and all out of my hands.

"What did they want with you in the magistrate's room?"

"They wanted the names of the gentlemen who come behind the scenes."

"Ha! I've been thinking of them."

"They took Warnham's name down too, Heartworth."

He frowned terribly.

"She's told me of him, too—he's villain enough for anything. I'll go directly to his villa at Richmond, and keep a watch upon the place."

"But I must do something. What shall I do?"

"Do you suspect anyone else?"

"The Honourable George Boddles—they put his name down."

"He's a drunken, dissolute fellow, but I

don't think that there's studied villainy enough in his composition ; and yet——"

" I'll go to his father."

" For what reason ?"

" I may find out where his son is."

" True."

He was hastening away, when I called him back.

" If you should hear anything of her, Mr. Heartworth, I hope you'll send to me—I'm very anxious."

" *If* I should hear anything."

So we parted, he to repair to Richmond, and I to wend my way to the town mansion of Lord Boddles.

I had great difficulty in obtaining an interview with Lord Boddles. All the servants dangling about the hall were quite Lord Boddleses themselves in plush and tags. Lord Boddles was very much surprised to see me, when I was finally ushered into his presence.

"What is it, man?" was his lordship's sharp inquiry.

"I suppose you remember me, my lord, as an actor at the George Theatre?"

"I have a faint idea," answered Lord Boddles—"man with snuff-box?"

"Yes, my lord."

"Well, what is the news?"

"Jenny Merton is missing, my lord."

"Merton!—Merton!—is that the girl who—oblige me by not spilling your snuff all over the place."

"Beg pardon, my lord."

"And do you really think that her absence is attributable to my—to the Honourable George Boddles?"

"I'm afraid to think, my lord," said I. "I have come to ask if you have seen the Honourable George Boddles lately, or if you would mind favouring me with his present address."

"The woman may have met with an accident—have you tried the hospitals?"

" All of them."

He appeared to reflect a moment.

"You can go," he said, suddenly look-ing up.

" Eh ?"

"You can go," he repeated, loftily. " I can't inform against my son. I have no-thing to say. It's all very dreadful ; but go away !"

" But——"

He rang the bell.

" But——"

The footman stood in the doorway wait-ing further orders.

"Show this man out," said his lordship ; " and you'll know him again—don't let him in any more. I don't want to see him—no one wants to see him. Stay !" He drew two sovereigns from his pocket, and pushed them along the table towards me. " Do not trouble your head about this affair," said he. " If the girl's gone away with my son, it's her own fault, and no business of yours."

"She has been stolen away, my lord."

"Pooh! pooh!" exclaimed Lord Boddles
—"young women are not stolen away in
the London streets now-a-days."

"She never went with her consent. I
won't take the sovereigns—I don't want
your money. Good morning, my lord.
May you never lose a child of your own!"

I did not wait for the footman to show me
the way, but marched indignantly past him,
and was soon crawling about the London
streets again, uncertain what to do.

I did not want to go home—I did not
know what course to adopt; I did not care
about living another day even. I did not
see any good in living—it was slow work.
I walked up and down before the mansion
of Lord Boddles, but saw no sign of him
or his honourable son. I got through all
my snuff before a church-clock in some back-
street struck four in the afternoon. I was
hunting for a few grains in the corner, when
some one touched me on the shoulder.

" What do you want here?"

" I'm not aware that it is any business of yours," I answered, staring at a lanky, yellow-faced individual beside me.

" But it *is* business of mine."

" Oh ! is it?"

" You were told not to interfere, and now here you are sneaking about this place. Why don't you go home?"

" Are you one of the——"

" Yes, I am. And now what have you been up to?"

" I have been to Lord Boddles."

He gave a snort of disapprobation.

" Do you mind going home?"

" What for?"

" Because I want you," said he; "because you're much better at home than interfering with my business; because I'll call upon you to-morrow, or the day after, and take you for a walk with me. Now go home, there's a good fellow."

His manner was so persuasive, and my

ideas were so confused, that I passively obeyed him. I took my usual post at the theatre in the evening. What a miserable evening that was! Warnham acted magnificently, and was called before the curtain at the end of every act. I could not get rid of my suspicions of that man, more especially when I found he was in a hurry to leave the theatre, and did not stop to wipe the rouge off his flabby face before he went. As for Heartworth, I saw nothing of him; he was not in the orchestra.

I could not keep from the Mertons the next day. I found him and his wife haggard and crestfallen through all their Indian-paint.

"Any news of Jenny?"

"No."

"No message from the police-office, Mr. Merton?"

"Not any."

They were the only words exchanged between us. It was some relief to call, so I

went round again after the theatre was
closed. The husband and wife were sitting
in their dark parlour.

" Any news of Jenny ?"

" Is that you, Whitedrop ?"

" Yes, it's Whitedrop."

" Ah ! there's no news."

" I hope you don't think that I had a
hand in it, now, Mr. Merton ?"

" No, I don't."

" Nor you, ma'am ?"

" I never did."

" Thank you, thank you," said I, " good
night."

" Good night," they answered ; and I
plodded home to my miserable garret.

I called several times the next day—no
news. When I reached home the last
time, the woman in the parlour informed
me that a tall gentleman had been inquiring
for me, and had left word that if I were
home within half an hour, I was to call at the
" King William " in the next street.

I started off at once, and found the police-officer, or detective, or thief-taker, or whatever he was, sitting in the tap-room, smoking a long clay pipe. He got up when he saw me. "Come on—how late you are! I told you to keep at home."

" Is there any good news?"

" I don't know whether it's good or bad yet. Come on."

" Which way?"

" We're going on the Croydon Road."

" Is she there?"

" We think so—somebody is."

" Let me run and tell——"

" Run and tell nobody," said the man. "You can identify her, that's all I care about Hi! hackney-coach there—hi!"

We were soon in a hackney-coach, and rumbling on towards Surrey. We went over Westminster Bridge, down the Kennington and Brixton Roads, at a funeral pace.

" How precious slow!" I remarked.

"There's no occasion for hurry. We can't do anything till after dark."

"Oh! dear."

"You mustn't be impatient. The gal has come to no manner of hurt or harm, but has been only under lock and key there since her kidnapping. Nobody's been nigh her but an old woman. When we're sure it is Miss Merton, we'll smuggle her off without a fuss."

"Without a fuss!—why, the law will never let this matter rest."

"N—no, perhaps not," he said, after a moment's thought.

"Is it far now?"

"It's a goodish distance."

"Do you mind stopping at the next general shop?"

"What for?"

"I should like some snuff. If there's any waiting about—I can't do without snuff."

We stopped at a little house near Streatham, where I filled my box. We dismissed the man and his fly at the corner of a green lane two miles from Croydon, and proceeded leisurely along. At a very lonely part of the lane we came upon a man in a smock frock.

" Anything new ?" asked my friend of this individual.

" Nothing new."

" All right. Have you the chaise ?"

" Over there."

After this desultory conversation they parted with a knowing wink at one another, and my companion and I proceeded further down the lane. When it was dark, and the stars shining overhead, he said,

" Now, Mr. Whitedrop, we're going on duty. Our plan is all arranged, and it's to be acted with ease and caution."

" There is no one to be taken into custody ?"

" I told you that before."

" Do you mean to say that a man is to steal away a young woman and not be punished for it?" I asked indignantly.

"Merton can prosecute if he choose—he has been advised not to do so."

"A pretty thing, indeed!"

"If we get away quietly we shall keep it out of the papers—they'll be glad to keep it out of the papers."

"They—who?"

He did not answer me. I pressed the question a second time, and he still maintained silence. I was bold enough to repeat the question once more, and he caught me by the arm, saying,

"Here's the house. Just hold your tongue a minute."

"If there's a hair of Jenny Merton's head injured——"

"She's all right enough," said he, "or we should not go to work in this fashion."

It was a large brick-built gloomy-looking mansion, standing at an angle of a broad carriage-road. It might have passed for a small nunnery or a private madhouse, and was admirably situated for either. The windows were closed and dark, and there was not a light to be seen glimmering in any portion of the edifice.

We went round to the back of the premises, and my companion, after bidding me wait for him by the high garden-wall, crossed the road and looked eagerly down a grass-grown lane. Presently he came back to me, saying,

"All right. Now then."

He tapped lightly with his knuckles at a small door in the wall.

"Is any one waiting for us?"

"The old housekeeper."

"Oh!"

The door was opened cautiously, and a sallow-faced woman admitted us.

"Has *he* come?"

"He drove down here about ten minutes ago."

"You don't mean that! Where is he now?"

"In his own room. He hasn't seen her yet."

"And the girl?"

"She's all right—she's waiting for you. There's a ladder for you under the bushes near the greenhouse. Look sharp."

The woman retreated towards the house. My friend began to steal cautiously along the gravel walks, and I followed in his footsteps. When we were near the house he stopped.

"Now, can you remain here for ten minutes, and keep very quiet?"

"I'll try."

"And in ten minutes come after me along that path and up the ladder."

"All right."

"You're sure you can swear to her?"

"Swear to Jenny Merton!" I cried, "I could swear to a tone of her voice—I could swear to her shadow—"

Before I had concluded my speech, the man had crept away. I kept my eyes fixed on the back of the house, and prayed silently for Jenny Merton's safety. I had not looked long in one direction before the shutter of a window on the first floor was unfastened, and a light gleamed from within the room as a signal. At the same moment a ladder was placed underneath, and I fancied that I could detect the black figure of my tall friend making his ascent. I saw him plainly when he reached the window, which was slowly opened as his head came level with the sill. He clambered into the room, the light was suddenly extinguished, and there was I alone in the garden, listening to imaginary sounds in the direction of the mansion, and half fancying—a pleasant thing to fancy in a strange place—that some one was creeping up behind me with a knife.

Five minutes had not passed before I lost my presence of mind, and began to fear that the officer had fallen into a trap, and that Jenny was farther from rescue than she had

ever been. I was far too nervous to remain
the allotted time in the garden, and after a
moment's hesitation I stole towards the
house, reached the ladder, ascended it, and
peered in at the window. It was a room
dark and tenantless. I crept in cautiously,
and began groping for a door in the opposite wall. I had just discovered it when the
sound of feet softly descending a flight of
stairs outside the chamber gave me hope
that all was right, and they were coming.

I stood back behind the door, and the
gleam of a dark lantern came athwart the
darkness.

" This way, Miss Merton."

" What place is this?—who brought me
here?—am I safe with you?"

" You have always been safe, for the
matter of that, miss," said the voice, in
reply, " but this is the most quiet way of
doing the job. He's a very great man,
you see, and my orders are to be cau-
tious."

"Is anyone waiting for me?" asked Jenny.

"A friend will be here almost directly."

"Mr. Heartworth?—my father?"

Heigho! she did not think of me! I gave vent to a deep sigh, and Jenny cried,

"What's that?" I stepped from behind the door.

"It's only poor old Whitedrop, Jenny Merton," I whispered. "I hope you don't think any the worse of him for not resting till he had found you, for not knowing a moment's happiness from the hour they stole you until now."

She sprung towards me, and flung her dear arms round my neck.

"I am so glad—I am so glad, my second father, my faithful, best of friends!"

She sobbed in her delight at meeting me again, and I sobbed too, only I made a greater noise about it, which offended the gentleman who had taken such pains to get Jenny away secretly.

"Come, none of this," grumbled he, "let's be off. What is there to stop for?"

She disengaged her arms—I could have let them cling there all my life!—and moved towards the window.

"Let me go first, and hold your hand," said the man; and, after putting the dark-lantern on the window-sill, he began to descend the ladder, guiding and directing Jenny, whose hand he held in his.

When they had reached the ground, I took my snuff-box from my pocket, and proceeded to enjoy a triumphant pinch over the mysterious enemy.

"Bring the lantern down, Mr. White-drop," called up Jenny's deliverer.

"Certainly."

"Look alive!"

Still holding the open snuff-box in my

hand, I raised one leg towards the window, when the room was suddenly lighted up, and I found myself dragged forcibly backwards by the tails of my coat.

"Villain! wretch! robber! where's the girl?—where's the girl?—where's the girl?"

I contrived to turn my head, and to behold Lord Boddles, purple and green with rage, dancing, jumping, foaming, swearing, and tugging me round the room by the tails of my coat. A servant, with two lights in his hand, stood by the door, aghast and open-mouthed.

"Put the lights down, and help me to secure this vagabond!" cried his lordship— "to break into my house—to—don't stand staring there, you fellow, don't!"

His lordship was too strong for me, and I felt my resistance growing weaker. I had only one hand at liberty—I did not like to drop my snuff-box.

"My lord, I never thought this of you!" gasped I—"my lord, I can't believe it——"

" You consummate rascal!—you con-
founded spy!—you——"

In our struggles I came, by a second
sharp twist, face to face with him again. I
felt that my strength and my coat-tails were
giving way together; I had a dim percep-
tion of a tall form bounding through the
window to my rescue; I lost all respect for
rank and title, I raised my snuff-box suddenly, and discharged its contents—the box
was brimming full—into his lordship's aristocratic eyes.

The effect was awful. Lord Boddles let
go, and flung his arms wildly in the air; he
spat; he sneezed; he groaned; he swore
worse than ever; he fought at an imaginary
opponent; he danced wildly about the
room; he wrung his hands; he kicked the
wall; he cursed his life and limbs, and me
and his eyes, for ever and ever.

" He has blinded me!—I'm stone gone!
—I'm a lost man!—I'm completely done
for!—it was a bottle of vitriol!—oh! Lord!

—oh! my poor eyesight!—oh! the devil!"

" You'd better let this matter rest, my lord," said the officer, who had returned to my side, "and not trouble yourself further. You'd better thank friends at court for this way of doing business. We're not supposed to know whose house this is, or who carried off the gal."

The servant, who had shown symptoms of a combative disposition, immediately turned down his sleeves, and put his hands into his pockets. His lordship continued to cut complicated figures about the room, rubbing his face and eyes, and sneezing.

" Oh! lor!—oh my—may I die if I don't have the man hanged for blinding me!—I can't see a bit!—WAS it vitriol?"

" Only snuff."

" Good God! to throw snuff in a person's eyes!—to go and—oh!"

He gave another leap, flung out his arms, and knocked the candles from his servant's hands. The police-officer pulled my sleeve, and, taking the hint, although I was desirous of giving the nobleman a severe lecture on his contemplated villainy, I got through the window, and descended the ladder. My companion quickly followed me. We hurried through the garden to a chaise waiting at the gate, with Jenny safe within it. I cried again to find her in safety, and she cried, too, and then away we went to London.

Towards London, her father, and Ned Heartworth.

I felt more miserable at every whirl of the wheels—I knew that she would give up the stage, marry Ned Heartworth, and leave me —a feeble and worn-out snuff-taker—to mourn for her for ever.

I was right—she married him, and they asked me to the wedding. I did not go—I contented myself with watching her enter the church from the corner of the street, and in crying and taking my snuff behind a post.

It was all over with me and my first love! I was very old to have a first love; and I should have become a rare laughing-stock at the George Theatre if I had told my secret, so I kept it to myself. But it was a true love for all that, and none the less deep and pure for having been fostered in a shabby wretch like me, without a word, a blush, a look to sustain it in its youth.

I fell ill after she was married—that was about the time Lord Boddles joined the Ministry—relinquished the stage, and took to starvation. I was passed from parish to parish, until I came to Fixature, where they have knocked me up a bed in the work-house to go off comfortably upon. But I am not inclined to die in a hurry, to oblige the overseers—I am lingering on the verge—I rally now and then, and wear out the patience of my watchers.

All but one, who comes to see me with a

little baby in her arms, and tells me how her dear Ned's mother has given up the business to her son, and how she is such a happy wife. Heaven bless her, she deserves to be!

A PROUD WIFE.

A PROUD WIFE.

CHAPTER I.

THE YOUNG COUPLE.

WE were scarcely more than boy and girl when Gilbert and I made up our minds to be married. Friends laughed at us after the usual fashion—a few condescended to advise us, I remember—but we thought that we knew our own minds better than they who sought to influence us, and we became man and wife. We were not children, though we had begun life early. Gilbert was alone in the world, and I had only a mother to study, whose

wishes went with my own, and who relied
too much on my judgment.

Gilbert and I were what the world called
a clever couple. We commenced life with
fair prospects ahead, and I thought that we
should both have the patience to wait for
fortune, and courage to strive through the
usual difficulties to obtain it. Gilbert was
only one-and-twenty when he married me,
and I was seventeen; but he was strong,
self-reliant, and energetic, I believed, and I
felt that his perseverance would make him
his name in good time. He was neither
weak nor vain. He saw the struggle with
the crowd before the race was won, and he
asked me very gravely whether I could be
content for years with a modest income and
a little house, knowing that contentment
would ever be with him, and not with his
surroundings. He had chosen engineering
for his profession. He had genius; he had
passed his examination with that high honour
which I was assured he would do; and

before he was three-and-twenty years of
age he had obtained a post of importance
that was likely to lead to something great
one day. Gilbert's income was not large at
first. He was to work up to greatness by
degrees, and there was a small addition of
seventy-five pounds a year on my side to
back us in our first start together.

I had begun to write for the magazines,
following at a distance in the footsteps of a
father who had killed himself by editor's
work it was said, and in my way I earned a
few pounds occasionally, almost against my
husband's wishes. He would grow eloquent
at times on the folly of my aspirations,
demonstrate to me plainly enough how impossible it was that I could ever be more
than a literary drudge, an " outsider " as he
termed it, and how it militated against his
dignity, and lowered him as " lord and
master," to see me working with himself for
home.

· Had we been blessed with children, I

might have reasoned with him in those early days of which I treat—those days of early struggles together, at which I look back longingly, and see how happy they were—but I knew how proud a man he was; and as he advanced slowly in his profession, so I drew back from mine—if I could ever call it mine—and let him work for both of us.

Yes, they were happy struggles after all. Our little household embarrassments were almost pleasant jesting when our hearts were young, and our friends were of our own seeking. We made no profession of being better off than we were; the few to whom we were well known understood our position, and believed in our advancement. We were ambitious, perhaps, but we kept our ambition to ourselves. I was the happier of the two possibly, for I was more easily contented, and I loved him better, I think that still, for all my great mistake. Had we remained poor all our lives, I should not have experienced one regret at linking myself with Gilbert Graham, unless his looks or words had been significant of his own disappointment. I say that now as fearlessly as I said it to him long ago, when we were rising in the world.

It was when we were beginning to rise that we encountered the first shadow, and this is how it came about:—

Gilbert, before he was four-and-twenty, had attracted the attention of the scientific public to a new theory of his own as regarded the construction of railway-bridges—a theory that drew attention to his name, and gained him some reputation amongst those whom in his career it was necessary to study.

We rose from that period. Gilbert's fame extended; men well known in the profession sought him out; old friends re-appeared, and fresh friends started up—or rather, those fair-weather acquaintances whom society calls friends. Let me mention one man in particular as the unwitting cause of my troubles—a man who meant well in his way, and who, after a fashion, liked and even respected my husband; but who, before I had cause for one reproach, cost me many a heart pang. Young wives will understand me, though only a few men will see fair reason for my first grief, when I say that he was my husband's friend more than he was mine. He sought Gilbert out, and—here is the secret—he took him away too much from home. He had been a schoolfellow of my husband's; he had risen in the world very rapidly, and was a rich man at six-and-twenty—rich, not by his own exertions, but by those of his uncle, who had died rich, and bequeathed to him the savings of long years. When Charles Ewell was a poor young man, I liked him better; it was his sudden wealth that seemed to set me against him, even before he stepped between Gilbert and me. It was not envy

at his sudden rise that disturbed me, for no
one congratulated him more from the heart
than Gilbert and I; it was his own new
manners, which Gilbert did not see, or
would not see, but which I was certain he
had assumed with the greater dignity which
his higher position had entailed upon him.
Society knows these men—these youths
who have not been born rich, but have had
riches thrust upon them—and does not like
them much, for all the court it pays them.
Wealth had not spoiled Charles Ewell more
than it would have spoiled most men; it
had altered his character, and given a new
turn to his thoughts, and it had rendered
him very objectionable to me. It has always been a mystery to me that Gilbert
was in this matter less clear-sighted than
myself; that with all his shrewdness and
his genius, he was so easily blinded by the
showy manners of his friend. He was the
last man to be affected by them in any way

that was prejudicial to his interest, but they changed him for all that, and they sowed the seeds of discontent within him.

Charles Ewell married well in the new sphere to which he had been raised, and we hired a brougham for the occasion, and went to his wedding, where his friends turned up their eyes at our horses, and laughed at our hack conveyance; as well they might, perhaps, for there was a great deal to laugh at, and we had had some fun from it ourselves driving to Hanover Square. We went, also, to Mr. Ewell's grand home in May Fair, in due course, to his stately dinners and still more stately balls, where the ladies looked down at my toilette, and Charles Ewell informed my husband what everything had cost in the room—what he had given for his pictures, what he was going to give for his new carriage. It was this parvenu habit, this common trait of the upstart, which irritated me most, because it impressed my husband a great deal, although he was not slow to smile at the restless vanity of his friend.

"I hope, Gilbert, your friend's grandeur will not set you against our little home," I said to him one night, when we were returning in a cab from one of Charles Ewell's dinner-parties.

He had been looking very thoughtfully over my head until my voice aroused him, then he started and laughed pleasantly.

"Oh, no, Ellen. His grandeur will not disturb my philosophy, though I would not mind changing houses with him."

"And wives?"

"No. I would take my wife to the big home, and she should shed more gladness round me there."

"Is there not gladness enough in the old home?" I asked, somewhat anxiously.

"To be sure there is. I am not envious —I am the last man to covet my neighbour's goods," he said lightly, "or to wish that little Charley's luck had fallen to my share. He is a good fellow, who deserves to succeed in the world. How welcome he made us, Ellen!"

"Yes, very welcome, certainly."

"I think that he paid us more court than he did the rest of his guests."

"Yes, he seemed anxious to show that our position in life made no difference to him."

"Ah! you speak satirically, Nell," he said. "You don't like Charles; and it is his grand home that seems to cast a shadow upon yours. You must not wish that we were better off yet awhile—presently we shall spread our wings, girl, and have a soul above our shabby little crib in the Wandsworth Road; and if we never have quite so many silver spoons and forks as Charley Ewell, still we will drop the electro-plate, and soar upwards."

This was turning my weapons against myself, and I could only smile at him, till the satire that was couched in his last words more forcibly suggested the new truth.

"I don't despise wealth, Nell," he continued, to my surprise, beginning again in his odd soothing manner towards me, and ending with the old bitterness towards a something or other that was not apparent. "I hope to grow rich in good time; to have as good a house, and keep as good a table as half those people whom we have met to-night, and whose only claim to be at Charley's place was the money that they had made in the City. By Jove! there was not an intellectual man or woman amongst them —they were a well-off lot, that's all. When my turn comes, see what friends I will have; the worst of it is, it can't come very soon."

I fancied that he sighed then; that it was his first sigh of regret at the position he occupied. We spoke of our own future the rest of the way home, and forgot Charles Ewell's rise to fortune. We spoke of our patience to wait, and courage to fight the

battle of life, with an undivided love to
keep us strong ; and when our small maid-
servant opened the door, we contrasted her
with Charles Ewell's plush-clad lackey, and
had our jest at the odious comparison.

But this was, after all, the beginning of
trouble. I date still the restless discontent,
the cruel mistakes and misconceptions, from
that night when the first sign was made that
Gilbert was dissatisfied with his progress
in life, despite all the success he had
achieved. He did not appear to have that
confidence in his own genius which carries a
man so forward into his future that he men-
tally rises above his present obscurity ; and
there ensued periods of re-action, when he
fancied that he was going back in the race,
and that fame and honour were never to
come to him. We had our cares when he
had become known to the profession as a
man of no common order of intellect. Fame
comes before money, as a rule, and I have
said that Gilbert had made many friends.

Gilbert's income might have been three hundred a year, not more, when we were still a young couple, and had changed, for the sake of position, into a larger house further west. Here we entertained, in a humble way at first, those friends who we thought valued us more for ourselves than for the entertainment we could afford them; or those friends, again, whom Gilbert asserted it was necessary to keep up with, even at a loss to ourselves, which was a theory I never wholly understood. And we did not save money; indeed, we had a hard struggle, at times, not to fall back into debt.

This was a greater struggle than Gilbert ever knew; for I concealed from him, in every way that I could, all the petty household cares which rose to the surface occasionally. I knew how much they would have disturbed him from his studies, and vexed him for days afterwards; and I did my best with our income, gratified by the knowledge that he was generally ignorant that at any period

of a past week there had been a sharp
corner to turn. Men, I suppose, never give
us credit for all the efforts we make to keep
down the housekeeping expenses. They
are engrossed with their business, and believe that there is no trouble in paying a few
tradesmen's bills. Now and then there was
a little *contretemps* to face, and an extra demand to make upon his purse; and then
Gilbert would do his best with me to stem
the tide, and would decline invitations, and
work hard at home, until our heads rose
above water once more. Once I fell ill—at
an inopportune period, when I should have
been at my strongest and best—and there
were nurses to hire, and a physician to con-
sult. I recovered to find that all things had
fallen into arrear, and that there were formidable bills to confront. Still we lived
down difficulties, worked hard, and were,
after all, tolerably happy in our way. There
were only a few up-hill years to surmount,
I told him, and then we could smile at our

past trials, and that happiness we had ever found in their midst, cheered by the love that had never grown less between us. He would grow eloquent in his turn then, paint his future as I had never dared to paint it for him, speak of me as his best adviser and truest friend, until Charles Ewell, or men like him, whom I need not introduce here, confronted him once more.

It was at my own house that the greatest blow fell at last. Mr. Ewell and his wife were there, and a few friends had been summoned to meet them. Gilbert had been inclined at first to extravagance in his ideas for our party, and I had had to combat his high notions, and to remind him that we were not yet rich enough to launch forth. It had been a successful little party in its way, I was inclined to believe, and everything had gone off well, though we had dispensed with a French cook and the highest-priced wines. I was a young wife, and proud of my home and husband, and it vexed me to know that Gilbert would half apologize to his friend Ewell for his small establishment and the general appurtenances around him whenever this grand young man favoured us with his company. On that night I detested him. I was a woman, not a heroine, and words that he uttered, and that I heard by chance, set my heart against him for ever.

"You don't come to see me, Charley, for my splendid dinners, or my old brands," Gilbert was saying as I passed him, "but for the sake of that old friendship which dates from the school-form."

"And for the sake of that friend's genius, which is so surely working its way, Gilbert —which we all see and respect," was the courteous answer enough.

My husband's saturnine mood asserted itself, and I could see his face shadow and his brow contract as he confessed to his friend all the opposition that was still in his path, just as he had confessed to me many times before, and been reasoned out of by my brighter prophecies. When I returned five minutes afterwards, Gilbert had concluded his long catalogue of the difficulties in the way of a man rising to independence in that profession which he had chosen for himself. Charles Ewell's reply I heard, and never forgave.

"Ah! but you don't think, Gilbert," he said, "how you have risen in comparison with the nine hundred and ninety-nine men of your own age and profession—risen in the face of every obstacle, with a house to keep up, and a wife to support, at an age when no man in your position, as a rule, thinks of taking such expenses on himself."

Gilbert should have spoken warmly here, for indirectly it had been implied that I was the barrier in the way of his advancement.

"Yes, I married early enough, Charley, but—I don't regret it," he added, after a pause, as though most men in his circumstances would have done so.

"As a single man, your income would have been ample for your wants," Ewell continued. "You could have travelled, and thus have benefited by the experience of all lands, instead of clinging to your own insular prejudices; and at thirty-five you might have chosen your wife from the first families in the land."

"I should have chosen Ellen," he said laughingly, and as I stole away I said Heaven bless him for that answer.

I was wretched for the remainder of the time Gilbert and Charles Ewell sat together. I could think only of my husband, and see on his gloomy brow, as I watched him from the distance, the shadow of the dangerous thoughts his friend had placed there. They sat and talked together in a low tone, forgetful of the company around them, and my nervous fancies, if they were merely nervous fancies, suggested that Gilbert's face grew darker every instant, and that he nodded his head more than once to the insidious reasoning of his friend.

Later in the night, when our guests had gone and we were alone together, the gloom still lingered on my husband's face, and no effort of my own could dissipate it.

"Has anything occurred, Gilbert, to annoy you this evening?" I asked.

"Nothing, Nell. It has been a very pleasant evening."

"I thought Charles Ewell might have said something to vex you," I said quietly.

"He is too good a fellow for that. What a pity it is, Nell, that you do not like him much! No man would do more to help me to rise in the world than he."

"Or to render you discontented with the present, from which you would escape."

I told him of the chance words that I had heard, and of the mortification that I had experienced in hearing them, till I broke down, like the sensitive woman that I was then. His arms were round me, and he drew

me to his side to reason with me—to assure
me that he was not dissatisfied with his success
in life; on the contrary, very grateful for it,
and that he was content to wait with me
patiently for the better fortunes that he
thought were on their way to us.

" Yes; but he spoke of your early marriage as a mistake," I said pertinaciously;
" of me as the clog upon your industry and
perseverance—the woman who retards your
progress, and is to hang round your neck a
dead weight for many years, and be always
a something that you must drag upwards
with yourself."

" No, he did not speak so forcibly as that,
Nell," he answered. " You never do Charley
justice—you never will. If he said that it
would have been easier for me to have saved
money as a single man than as a Benedick,
why, there was no great harm, and a little
truth in the assertion."

" Yes; and that assertion implied the
hindrance that I had been to you. Oh,

Gilbert! and you think that too—you see
that without me you might have been a
richer man, and nearer the mark at which
you aim."

"What does it matter? I am satisfied,
Ellen. I have nothing to regret. I have
been lucky in my profession, and in the wife
who supports me in my efforts."

So we became reconciled to the present
again, and I believed all that he had told me
for a few days—a few weeks until a new
change came over him, which I did not
comprehend, and yet which I could only
guess was connected with myself.

There was the heavy look upon his face
that I had seen on the night Charles Ewell
dined with us, and spoke of me as Gilbert's
dead weight, and I connected it truly enough
with the man who called himself my husband's friend. It was in taxing Gilbert with
the change in him that the truth escaped.

"You have seen Mr. Ewell lately, Gilbert,"
I said.

" Yes, how did you know that ?"

" I fancied that you must have met him, for, forgive me for the thought, I fancy that you are never your old self afterwards."

" It is an ungenerous thought, Ellen."

" He has spoken of me again. Perhaps he has——"

" Pardon me, but he has not mentioned your name," said Gilbert quickly. " See how you leap to conclusions that are un-worthy of you, in your strange dislike to him. He has offered me, Ellen, a lucrative post abroad."

" Indeed, and you——"

" Have declined it. It was impossible, under the circumstances, that I could accept it."

Under the circumstances that he was married, that it would necessitate breaking up home, perhaps, and leaving me !

" Tell me all about the post which has been offered you, Gilbert ?"

Then I heard all the truth, and guessed

that the first great disappointment of his life had come. A post had become vacant abroad, a post of some hardship, connected with the construction of a foreign railway, necessitating not only considerable talent, but requiring strength of constitution to combat an insidious climate, and much strength of character to fight against the opposition which was to be encountered there. All save the strength of character Gilbert possessed, perhaps; but the whole scheme did not appear to me, despite the advantages which were proffered, a project worth pursuing, or worth sinking all the chances which remained to him in England, and would come to him in time. I said this, but he would not understand my reasoning—rather grew irritable under it, as though he had outgrown my advice, or did not care for it. There had been a chance of sudden advancement; there was the novelty of adventure in it, if all Charles Ewell's statements were correct, and there were opportunities of making money indirectly in a variety of ways. It did not matter that my husband's genius might prove equally remunerative here—he had lost much of his faith in himself lately.

"Why not accept this post?" I said at last.

"Oh! Nell, I am sure that you would not like me to leave you for a year—probably two."

"I will try to bear your absence, if you think it is necessary for your advancement in life—if you are dissatisfied with your position here."

"This is a snail's progress. I may be well off years hence, when a dozen people have died to make room for me. I may be talked of by my set when I am old and feeble, not before."

"You are not content, then, with your present position?"

"No—I am not," he confessed.

"Had you been a single man, you would have gone?" I asked.

"I should not have hesitated one instant."

"Then return to Charles Ewell, and tell him that, if it be not too late, you will accept the proposal that he has made you. Become a single man for a year or two again; you will never forgive yourself if you hear of another man's success in that sphere which you would have chosen—you will never forgive me."

Heaven knows whether I meant him to jump so readily at my offer—whether I had not rather designed it in my heart as a test of his affection, and had expected him to say that he would remain content with his wife, and with the position that he had secured, rather than dash at the chances offered him abroad. He did not dream of asking me to accompany him—he feared for my health, I knew; but still I would have risked my life to be with him rather than have remained alone in England. I had to make this offer for myself, and he said that it was impossible, and that, however I might desire it at the present time, I should know no happiness hereafter, and be one incessant source of responsibility to him. Perhaps he was right, but I only thought that he was secretly anxious to be gone, despite his affectation of wavering, his talk of home and me. But I would have shared all trials with him, oh, so cheerfully! It would have been a greater satisfaction to have met troubles with him, to have lightened his cares by my presence, if that presence could have done it, than to have remained at home in security and ease without him. And he spoke of me as a difficulty, never as a helpmate and a comforter, as I knew that I had been in our English home together, and my pride rose at last and held me tongue-tied.

He went away to seek Charles Ewell;

he found the appointment had been almost
promised to a second person ; he spent the
next two days in excitement and suspense
which rendered him more churlish and irritable than I had ever known him, and he
broke forth into a childish delirium of joy
when the news came that it was not too
late, and that the post was open to him
still.

It was all settled ; Gilbert was to relin-
quish a good home, a certainty of rising in
the world, and a wife who loved him very
dearly, for the chance of a fortune abroad.
I did not believe that he would attain it,
though I would not damp him with my
prophecies. It was arranged that I was to
go back to my mother, and that the home
wherein we had been happy together was
to be broken up for ever. Presently Gilbert was to return, and with his riches to
build up a new home for us both—he said
so, but I did not answer to his promise.
The tears were in my eyes, and I could not

see the new life beyond for the mist that gathered there, and shut out the fairer prospect which his hopes portrayed.

END OF THE FIRST VOLUME.

LONDON : PRINTED BY MACDONALD AND TUGWELL, BLENHEIM HOUSE.